Phoenix Senior English Guides

Robert Frost

FRANCES RUSSELL MATTHEWS

PHOENIX
EDUCATION

PHOENIX
EDUCATION

First published in Australia in 1999

PHOENIX EDUCATION PTY LTD
PO Box 197, Albert Park 3206
Tel: (03) 9699 8377 .Fax: (03) 9699 9242
PO Box 3141, Putney 2112
Tel: (02) 9809 3579 Fax: (02) 9808 1430

ISBN 1 875695 86 9

Text design and page make-up by Graphic Divine
Cover design by Sharon Carr
Cover marbling by Galen Berry
Printed in Australia by Shannon Books

Contents

How to use this book

This book provides you with a structure for getting to know the work of the American poet Robert Frost. In it you will find a brief biography of his life and a summary of the major influences on the development of his poetry, a summary of some of his most important ideas, themes and techniques, a guide to developing your own response to important examples of his work, some hints on the analysis of individual poems, and a guide to preparing for and writing effectively in exams.

Chapter 4 'The poems in close-up' offers you three levels of response so that you can confidently develop your *own* response and understanding of Frost's work.

- **Your first response**: This is your record of your initial impressions on first reading and thinking about the poem. You may like to write notes as you read: jot down possible themes, and note effective, surprising or challenging imagery. Observe the effectiveness of individual sounds or phrases. Note the use of rhyme. Try to 'feel' the way the rhythm or metre works. Draw some basic conclusions about the poem: Is it sad? Happy? Provocative? Challenging? Does it ennoble humanity or criticise it? Is it joyful at the nature of life or thoughtful about its challenges? Does it use colour? Is there an obvious symbol?

- **A closer analysis**: This provides you with a structured, focused analysis of each idea in turn and asks questions that challenge your thinking.

- **Your second response**: Take this opportunity to write at length on the poem. Refer to the text of the poem to select quotes which effectively support your argument. Try to write a coherent discussion on one of the suggested topics — or on one of your own. You can do it! This is your first step to taking hold of the poem and successfully meeting the challenge of its ideas.

Remember: use this text to develop your own ideas. View all that it says critically!

A guide to the analysis of poetry

Poetry is sound with meaning which challenges the imagination. It is a very specialised form of communication; its uniqueness depends on:

- a sensitivity to the effect of individual sounds, individual words and particular word combinations
- an expression of deeply felt emotions and feelings
- an intensity of thought and a consciousness of thought patterns
- a selectivity of subject matter in order to focus on particular themes
- a structural dependency (often) upon particular poetic forms

The analysis of any **poem** requires you to:

- identify the subject matter and the specific focus of its presentation
- explore the **themes developed** through the subject matter
- respond to the **language** used by the poet to encode thoughts, feelings, nuances and suggestions
- develop a sensitivity to the effectiveness of sound and sound patterns
- have an awareness of the individual treatment of an individual genre, where one is used as the structural and thematic base of the poem
- apply the principles of good essay writing: understand the question, and write about it with a specific focus in an well-organised structure

Understanding a poem

To successfully read and understand any poem:

- Take notice of the title (if there is one) – this will define the subject matter of the poem or the poem's thematic focus.
- Create a context for your deeper thoughts about the poem by reading it quickly to gain a first impression.
- Make notes the impact of the first and last words of each line – they often focus on key ideas.

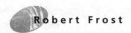
- Read the poem again – carefully, analytically and out loud. Remember that poetry is essentially sound with meaning.
- Note the impact of the poetic language – identify the particularly effective sounds and words; be aware of sound patterns and of the feelings and sensitivities these evoke in the reader.
- Identify the obvious meaning, then look for implied meaning(s).
- Read the poem again to consolidate your appreciation of its meaning.
- Identify a hierarchy of themes – do not expect the themes to be developed equally.
- Assess how the use of imaginative language, poetic imagery and figures of speech contributes to the portrayal and expansion of the meaning.
- Be sensitive to the use of setting and atmosphere as symbols of the main themes.

Identifying poetic themes

In order to identify poetic themes, you need to identify the ideas, attitudes, feelings and philosophy are presented by the poet through the subject matter of events, characters and philosophy – whether personal, religious or social.

Remember that while some themes are unique to every poem in the personal focus given to their presentation by the poet, many themes are universal to all poetry. These universal themes include:
- the nature of love and its associated happiness, trials and sadness
- the patterns of the natural world, including the cycle of the seasons
- our place in relationship with the natural world
- the beauty and horror to be found in nature
- humanity's own nature
- the nature of idealism and its defeat in the face of reality
- the special world view of young people
- the losses, wisdom, disenchantment and resignation of old age
- the corruption of humankind
- the pain and trauma of grief
- the powerlessness of humankind against time, war and passion
- the futility and brutality of war
- the value of ordinary lives
- the tensions that beset ordinary lives
- the value of solitude and the pain of loneliness
- the transience of all things – the inevitability of decay and of death for all living things
- the reality of pain and the horror of death
- the power and nature of arrogance and the quiet strength of humility
- the strength of anger and the power of forgiveness

- the special state of motherhood
- the power of the human imagination
- the often destructive power of religion yet the human need for faith
- the eternal struggle between good and evil
- the value and the emptiness of patriotism
- the beauty of the landscape
- the relentless power of natural forces – rain, frost, snow, wind, sun
- the anonymity and stress of urban life
- the bonds of our common humanity
- the often indifference of politics to the real needs of humankind
- humankind's struggle to communicate
- the power of despair
- estrangement and isolation
- the value of independence

Know your technical terms

Understand the basic form of the poem you are studying. This will give you a basis for your analysis and provide a guide to the nature of the ideas and the type of emotions to be examined in it.

If you understand the basic techniques of the poem you can discuss its style and, more importantly, the integration of style and meaning.

Develop your own working analytical vocabulary through the effective use of technical terms. Some important technical terms for you to identify and understand are listed here:

allegory: literally 'other meaning'. In allegory, characters, incidents and/or setting operate on many levels. What is depicted as the life of an individual may represent a universal statement about the life of Everyman. The story of a wanderer may represent the journeys made by all people living out their individual lives.

alliteration: literally 'more letters'. Alliteration is the repetition of sounds (mostly consonants), usually at the beginning of words or stressed syllables. It creates atmosphere, and emphasises the poem's ideas and feelings by the sounds it interweaves in the poetic line.

archetype: a character, an image or storyline which is found repeatedly in myth and throughout literary tradition: the mother or nurturer as the strength of the family; the scapegoat and the journey from life into the world of death; and the antagonist and destroyer are some of these.

assonance: literally 'the answer to'. It is the correspondence (or near correspondence) in two words of the stressed vowel, and sometimes also of the following vowels. This method of creating patterns in sound is a common feature

of English verse, and often adds dramatic intensity to a poem, giving it a coherence of sound that is married to the coherence of ideas.

ballad: the traditional ballad has given modern poetry a sense of drama, a vivid exploitation of dialogue, a simple stanza form of four lines, a sense of lilting rhythm and an appreciation of rhyme in reinforcing the metrical and semantic patterns. A ballad opens abruptly as the setting and the action are swiftly and economically drawn. It often repeats key ideas or key events – often in a refrain.

blank verse: unrhymed verse, often written in iambic pentameters. It mimics natural speech, although it is a little more sophisticated.

conceit: a figure of speech which establishes a startling contrast between two apparently quite dissimilar ideas or images.

dramatic monologue: the spoken expression of the poet as the main character. The speaker addresses one or more people who are not heard in the poem but whose reactions are responded to or foreshadowed by the speaker. The speaker's character is revealed by the content and structure of what he or she says.

elegy: a formal lament for the death of an individual, or for human mortality and the transience of all things that are meaningful for humankind.

enjambment: the flow-on of one poetic line into the next without a break, and the consequent flow-on of ideas and feelings.

epic: a long narrative on a serious subject, told with a sense of ceremony in formal speech which is elevated in style. The setting is a comprehensive one spanning hell, earth and heaven. The action is heroic and often involves superhuman feats. The main character faces many difficulties.

epigram: a very short poem of two or three lines which makes a succinct, often witty comment on a subject.

figurative language: the imaginative use of language so that it has more than a literal meaning. Personification, simile and metaphor are examples.

heroic couplet: rhyming pairs of lines, each with five units each consisting of an unstressed syllable followed by a stressed syllable. Heroic couplets were used by Shakespeare to round off sonnets.

imagery: the imaginative pictures created by the words of a poem. Imagery appeals to all five senses – sight, sound, taste, touch and hearing. Imagery is also used to describe the effect of figurative language.

lyric: the term originates from early Greek songs rendered to the accompaniment of a lyre. It is now used to describe a relatively short, non-narrative poem presenting the thoughts and feelings of a single speaker. The speaker may be alone or, in a dramatic lyric, address another person.

When analysing a lyric, you are often tempted to identify the first-person speaker of the poem with the poet himself. Even those lyrics which evoke situations close to the poet's own experience do not do make this simple equation. The speaker of a lyric is an artistic invention and may have nothing in common with the poet at all.

The lyric genre is an appropriate form for the expression of a brief mood or state of mind as well as for the expression of a complex state of mind. Subclasses of lyric include the sonnet, elegy, ode and dramatic monologue forms.

metaphor: a comparison of one kind of thing, quality or action to another by directly stating that it *is* the other thing. It is a compact form of imagery which expands in the imagination. It has a philosophical and intellectual confidence and often introduces a sense of drama.

metre: the regular rhythm given to a poem by the stresses of its words in isolation and in combination. Metre is the backbone or scaffolding of a poem's meaning.

poetic diction: the combination of the words, phrases and figurative language of a poem. Poets often give individual characters their own distinctive diction. Their work is often characterised by favourite words or turns of phrase.

pun: a play on words to create a joke with meaning.

ode: a long lyric poem, serious in subject, formal in style and complicated in verse pattern. Odes are poems of praise or contemplation.

onomatopoeia: word patterns and word combinations whose sound recreates the sound it denotes. Frost makes particularly effective use of this device.

pastoral: traditionally a Greek poem written about the lives of shepherds and shepherdesses. Today, the term is applied to any poem which celebrates the joys of simple lives led by working people. Many of Frost's poems have a pastoral quality in their documentation of individual experiences.

personification: the technique of assigning the qualities and feelings of a living being to an inanimate object. It thereby provides an imaginative expansion of the poem and is often a key to a poet's exploration of the meaning of universal themes.

rhyme: the agreement of two metrically accented syllables in their vowel sounds and final consonants.

rhyme scheme: the pattern created by rhyme in the last words of each line. The pattern is described by giving a letter of the alphabet (*a b c ... z*) to each particular end-rhyme.

satire: a satirical poem uses comedy as a weapon to promote laughter at the object, person or event so derided. Through such laughter, readers are brought to the recognise their own potential to commit the same error or to demonstrate the same egotistical action.

simile: a comparison between two different things using 'like' or 'as'.

sonnet: a one-stanza lyric poem of fourteen lines, linked by a complex rhyme scheme. Love was the traditional subject, but they are now used to deal (either seriously or even comically) with almost any subject in an elevated, formal way. Sonnets are characterised by intensity of thought and, often, a sense of drama.

Understanding poetic metre

A poetic line is a row of syllables. Each syllable has a metrical value – a degree of emphasis – which, when scanned, will give you the metrical pattern of the line. The simplest pattern is that between stressed and unstressed syllables. Together these provide the metrical scheme of the poem.

Stress is emphasis, the degree of loudness given to the articulation of any sound. Additional contributory factors are pitch; the duration or length of the sound; and the weightiness given to the sounds by the individual consonants. The relative amount of stress given to each syllable reflects the modification of its normal pronunciation by logical demands of the ideas being presented and their emotional emphases.

The simplest means of marking stress patterns is the use of a slanting stroke to mark the major stresses in a line and a cross to mark the weak stresses. The patterns created by these strong and weak stresses fall into groups called metrical feet which are made up of a combination of two or three syllables, only one of which is stressed.

The kinds of metrical feet thus created have names adopted from classical sources. The most important are shown below:

Name	Syllable pattern	Written as:	Example
iamb	unstresssed–stressed	X/	*intense*
trochee	stressed–unstressed	/X	*feather*
anapaest	unstressed–unstressed–stressed	XX/	*refugee*
amphibrach	unstressed–stressed–unstressed	X/X	*resemble*
dactyl	stressed–unstressed–unstressed	/XX	*magical*

These metrical patterns allow us to formally characterise the poet's use of the rhythms of everyday speech. The most common metrical pattern is the iambic pattern. The next most common is the other two-syllable pattern, the trochee. Any variation from the usual iambic metre will provide metrical emphasis to the words (and therefore the ideas) which are differently and unexpectedly accented. Other elements of variety are added to the poetic line by:

- a pause in the middle of the line (marked by a dash or a full stop or colon) known as *caesura*
- the patterns of sound created by the use of rhyme, usually a combination of assonance and alliteration
- the use of enjambment
- the interweaving of monosyllabic and trisyllabic words within the standard iambic line
- the use of couplets (two adjacent rhymed lines) which provide distinct units of sense

A biography of Robert Frost

His parents' marriage

Robert Frost's father, William Prescott Frost Jnr, was born in New Hampshire in 1850 into a family that could trace its roots back to Puritan New England. William Frost rebelled violently against his heritage to become a gambler, drinker, philanderer and schoolteacher. In March 1873 he married Isabelle Moodie, a woman with fanatical religious beliefs who was seven years older than himself. Thereafter, Will pursued a career in journalism and Belle, as Isabelle became known, contributed to the newspaper he ran.

Their son, Robert Frost, was born in 1874 – nine years after the end of the Civil War, when Ulysses Grant was President. He was named Robert Lee Frost after the failed Confederate General Robert E Lee, and years later smarted at what he believed to have been his early arrival in his parents' marriage and his being named after a man whose bravery as a soldier, though unquestioned, was not matched by his statesmanship.

The Frost's marriage was a bitterly unhappy one due largely to Will's dissolute behaviour and failed political aspirations, and Belle's retreat into the isolation of religious mysticism as a way of easing her pain. Frost was bitterly disillusioned by what he felt was his mother's tragedy in loving an undeserving man.

Growing up in San Francisco

Frost grew up in San Francisco. In 1874, when the Frosts arrived there, it was a bustling cosmopolitan port notable for its corruption and lawlessness, and large immigrant population. His childhood was marked by terrifying brutality from his father and a compensating overindulgence by his mother who nevertheless gave him his literary roots.

Before he had left his childhood behind, he was very familiar with the Bible, serious 19th-century books such as Fenimore Cooper's *The Last of the Mohicans*, Thomas Hughes' *Tom Brown's Schooldays*, Jules Verne's *The Mysterious Island*, the lyrics of the Scottish poet Robert Burns, and Scottish folklore and history – all of which provided him with rich sources for his own writing.

Frost was baptised a Presbyterian but attended Unitarian Sunday School and eventually followed his mother into the Swedenborgian faith – a religion with a strong spiritualist component. The lasting effect of the latter is recorded in Frost's own accounts of his being haunted, even into adulthood, by the mysterious supernatural voice of unseen beings who brought messages he could not interpret. Its influence can also be recognised in the mystical element of his poetry with its emphasis on the instruction – albeit imperfect – about the meaning of existence to be gained from the individual's interaction with nature.

Frost's education was spasmodic. A stomach-ache lasting three years saw him miss first, second and third grades in exchange for being taught to read and write by his mother. Much of his schooling was informally obtained from time spent on the streets of San Francisco and in its saloons.

The move east

In May 1885, his father died of tuberculosis leaving Belle and her two children, Robert and Jeanie, penniless. The family moved to Lawrence, a mill town in Massachusetts only to be reviled by Robert's grandparents as having caused the death of their only son.

To support herself and her children, Belle obtained a teaching position in a small school in Salem in New Hampshire. Robert and Jeanie at last began their formal education in their mother's classes but were humiliated by her poverty and by her lack of confidence. The latter forced the family to move to four different schools until, in 1890, Frost called a railway slum in Lawrence home.

In 1888, Frost enrolled in Lawrence High school and began a classical program of study which included Latin, Greek and European history. He developed an interest in reading the poetry of Shelley, Keats, Poe and Arnold. He wrote his first poem, 'La Noche Triste', which was published in the High School Bulletin in April 1890. In the summer of 1892 he graduated and promptly fell in love with Elinor White, his co-valedictorian. After the performance of their own secret marriage ceremony, Frost used Shelley's poem 'Love's Philosophy' to unashamedly bend Elinor's will to his – a moment of sexual ruthlessness which he later wrote about in 'The Subverted Flower' and which may have contributed to the future difficulties of their relationship.

Although he passed the entrance exams to Harvard, Frost went instead to Dartmouth College. He stayed there only a short time before leaving its victimisation and bullying behind to join his mother in her school at Methuen. This decision cost him a professional job and led him to many years of poverty and misfortune. The only experiences he had to draw on were early years of short-lived menial jobs including selling newspapers, working in a shoe factory, as a handyman and errand boy, a fruit picker, mill worker and, in Salem, as a schoolteacher. They provided him with a worldly education in his association with the rural and urban poor, and years later with many subjects for his poetry, including 'The Lone Striker'.

In 1894 his grandfather gave him an endowment to support his poetry writing for one year. In fact, twenty years passed before he published his first book of poetry in 1913. For all its shortcomings, Dartmouth College introduced Frost to Palgrave's anthology of poetry *The Golden Treasury*, whose collected poems of major poets was to provide a vital source of literary allusion and poetic stimulus, to Thomas Hardy's novels, and to the New York periodical *The Independent*, whose brother and sister editors, William and Susan Hayes Ward, published his first professional poem 'My Butterfly' on 8 November 1894, and six more of his poems between 1896 and 1908.

Attempted suicide in Dismal Swamp

In the autumn of 1894, Frost resumed his pursuit of Elinor White. In response to her rejection of his advances he travelled, in November of the same year, over 1400 kilometres from Lawrence to North Carolina, where he walked 16 kilometres into Dismal Swamp in a pretended suicide attempt. In doing so, he echoed the actions of the spurned lover of Thomas More's poem 'The Lake of Dismal Swamp' and entered that nightmarish realm popularised by Longfellow's 'The Slave of Dismal Swamp'. In part response to the bravado of his action, Elinor agreed to become Frost's wife. Frost celebrated his experience of the attraction of suicide in his poem 'Into My Own'.

Marriage and children

Frost and Elinor were married on 19 December 1895 in a classroom of Belle's school where Frost was to teach, and in 'Paul's Wife' Frost celebrated his feelings for his new wife. Their first child, Elliott, was born on 25 September 1896, followed by Lesley on 28 April 1899, three more children – a son, Carol, and daughters Irma and Marjorie – between 1902 and 1905, and a sixth child,

daughter Elinor Bettina in June 1907 who was to live for only two days. Their marriage was troubled – Elinor was sickly and a poor housekeeper, and Frost doubted her fidelity; the poem 'The Middletown Murder' expresses his suspicions on this point.

In September 1897, Frost enrolled in Harvard. He was 23. There he studied Latin and Greek, philosophy, and English composition but resigned from his sophomore class in March 1899. The formal metre and forms of classical poetry were to influence Frost's work for the remainder of his life. He developed a liking for pastoral poetry, rural subjects and settings, social criticism, the brevity of the Greek poets as well as their use of concise couplets, phrases with a striking immediacy, and love of concentrated thought.

All these were brought to express Frost's woe at the deterioration of his marriage after Elliott's death on 8 July 1900. 'Home Burial' (1914) records the bitterness that existed between Elinor and Frost after this tragedy.

A farm and apple orchard of his own

In September 1900, the Frosts moved to a farm in Derry, New Hampshire, complete with apple orchard and its own small brook. (Years later he was to return there and write in 'Directive' about his bitter disappointment at how much the cradle of his poetry had been allowed to run down.) Abandoning teaching, Frost became a farmer and developed that close acquaintance with the impoverished New England countryside that is reflected in the details of the rural settings and in the behaviour of the rural characters of his poems. He was most successful at raising chickens and growing apples, and supplemented the income these pursuits provided by selling a number of short stories between 1903 and 1905.

The decade of independent but isolated farming life that followed allowed Frost to indulge his love of English literature. The writers and poets who came under his scrutiny were innumerable: Horace, Virgil, Wordsworth, Shakespeare, Milton, Mark Twain, Charles Darwin, Catullus, Turgenev, Henry James, Waldo Frank, Sherwood Anderson, Robert Herrick, Sinclair Lewis, Ernest Hemingway, Byron, Shelley, Keats, Browning, Arnold, Thomas Hardy, Rudyard Kipling and Francis Thompson. This was also a productive time for Frost's writing of his own poetry, much of which unashamedly drew on these sources and recorded his indebtedness by its many literary allusions. Undoubtedly too in this time, he revisited the poem which had inspired him to write poetry: William Collins' 'How Sleep the Brave'.

The most influential poet, however, was Wordsworth. Frost emulated him in his preferred poetic subjects of situations and incidents experienced by ordinary people living out their everyday lives; in his diction which emulated the simple rhythms and words of the common colloquial speech of rural men and women, and in his exploration by its means of the deep, elemental emotions of their hearts. In all he found an illustration of the laws of nature and of the cosmos.

The works of novelist and poet Thomas Hardy reinforced and added to Wordsworth's and the other Romantic poets' influence on Frost's own writing. From Hardy, Frost learnt the importance of atmosphere and was awakened to the tragic passing of rural life and its simple values, and to the bleakness of a universe ruled by a force at best indifferent to the struggles of humankind. More positively, Hardy taught Frost the importance of character and story, and the powerful drama of human emotions. Hardy also provided him with a model for recording nature with a fine eye for detail. A mark of Hardy's influence is that his titles are the most echoed in the titles of Frost's own poems, and his images the most used.

Frost's poetic theory

From Shakespeare (especially *Hamlet*), Milton ('Comus') and Pope ('An Essay on Criticism' (1711), Frost developed his own poetic theory that sound in poetry is much more important than sense; that tone and cadence matter much more than individual words.

A return to teaching

The inadequacy of his farming and literary income drove Frost in 1906 to return to teaching at Pinkerton Academy in Derry. He quickly developed a reputation for the innovative teaching of English literature but by 1911 the pressure of work saw his health deteriorate.

He took up a part-time position at Plymouth Teachers' College. This allowed him time to recuperate and to write, yet by 1912 he was ready for a grand change. In August 1912 the family moved to London.

England and the publication of *A Boy's Will*

The English welcomed the Frosts. Two months after his arrival, Frost handed his first collection of poetry, *A Boy's Will*, to Mme M. L. Nutt who included it in her series of modern poets published in April 1913. The volume was dedicated to Elinor (as were all but one of Frost's works) and took its title from lines in Longfellow's poem 'My Lost Youth'.

Its thirty-two autobiographical poems, loosely tracing the course of a youth's maturing view of the world, are rooted in the New England landscape and heavily dependent on classical pastoral models. The volume received warm reviews.

In April 1914, the Frosts moved into a picturesque cottage built in Shakespearean times in Leddington, near Dymock. There they enjoyed the company of convivial literary friends such as Rupert Brooke, John Drinkwater and Edward Thomas. The latter was to become his closest friend and confidante. Not long after, in May 1914, Frost's second collection of poems, *North of Boston* was published.

North of Boston is published

The sixteen poems of *North of Boston* are dramatic dialogues, often witty and ironic, exploring Frost's favourite themes of self-reliance and individualism in a regional environment of isolation, decay and desolation. Captured in the authentic rhythms and rural simplicity of a poetic diction which embodies the principles of natural poetic language espoused by Wordsworth in the preface to his *Lyrical Ballads* is a certain way of life which Americans readily identified with: a frontier-like struggle with the land and its controlling elements encompassing all the pain, and emotion and psychological actuality of real experience lived by real people. From this point, Frost's poetry is characterised by a common language and a natural voice.

On 13 February 1915, the Frosts returned to New York and to enthusiastic reviews of the new work. In April 1917, Frost's best friend, Edward Thomas, was blown apart by a German shell. Frost never forgot their year of special friendship and dedicated his *Selected Poems* (1923) to Edward's memory and wrote four poems about him: 'The Road Not Taken', 'A Soldier', 'To E. T.' (Frost's only elegy) and 'Iris by Night'.

Mountain Interval is published

In November 1916, Frost's third book of poetry, *Mountain Interval*, was published. Several of the poems in this collection drew on Frost's Gloucestershire experience. In form the poems were varied: some draw on the pastoral tradition; some are rhymed lyrics; others are dramatic narratives in blank verse; there is one ballad and three children's poems. The ideas they present are darkly Frost: isolation, fear, human suffering, sudden violence, horror and death set amidst the changing seasons. The collection was well received, and Frost's reputation was now established. His response was to embark on a war with other poets to preserve it while he cultivated for himself a public persona of the farmer poet.

Farms, teaching and public readings

In June 1915, Frost bought a farm in the White Mountains of New Hampshire. Typically, the accommodation it provided the family was basic and the life simple. In 1920, he moved on to a similar existence in Vermont and in November of the same year to a farm near Arlington. (In all, the family was to move home almost forty times!) Frost devoted his time to college teaching, public readings and the promotion of his poetry, having become professor of English in Amherst College, Massachusetts, in January 1917, and oscillating largely between this institution and the University of Michigan (1921–23), Harvard and Dartmouth College. His academic appointments were short-lived as he moved from one to the other, seeking better-paid positions which nevertheless allowed him time to write.

New Hampshire is published

On 15 November 1923, Frost's fourth book of poetry, *New Hampshire*, was published. It is divided into three sections; the first containing the title poem; the second longer, blank verse narrative poems and the third, thirty shorter, rhymed lyrical poems. The themes were typical: the beauties of New Hampshire; humankind's place in the cosmos; the dignity and harsh reality of farm work; the parallel between the nature and demands of farm work and of poetry writing; the bitterness of life; the supernatural, the destructive forces of passion and hatred; the invaluable education to be obtained through experience of rural life rather than of formal education; the mutability of all things; the tempting nature of suicide; the evasiveness of the abstract truths of existence. Again, Frost's poems were well received and the invitations for speaking engagements increased. Frost now had an adoring public. Meanwhile, America grappled with the restrictions of Prohibition.

A brief move to France and the publication of *West-Running Brook*

At the beginning of August 1928, Frost sailed with Elinor and his youngest daughter Marjorie to Le Havre in France. He was, however, an unhappy French tourist, and moved quickly on to England. The family returned home to America in November 1928. In that same month, Frost's fifth volume, *West-Running Brook*, was published. The collection was uneven in achievement and the poems met with mixed reviews.

Return to America, family tragedies and the publication of *A Further Range*

In the late 1920s and early 1930s, Frost suffered a series of family tragedies: daughter Lesley's marriage broke down when she was pregnant with her second daughter; Marjorie had a nervous breakdown and contracted tuberculosis only to die due to complications arising from childbirth; Irma ran away from her husband; Lillian's health declined; Elinor had a heart attack. The Frosts moved south to Florida to soak up the sun.

In the remainder of the 1930s, Frost ignored the growth of crime in America, Prohibition and the Depression, holding fast to his conservative political views. This contributed in part to the low-key reception of his next collection, *A Further Range.*

Frost's achievement in *A Further Range* was again uneven, but its range across a variety of poetic genres – including satire, ballad, epigram, epithalamium, dramatic monologue, comedy, sonnet, pastoral and narrative – attested to his technical skill. Their subject matter was met coolly by the critics for being out of touch and reactionary.

The death of Elinor

On 20 March 1938, Elinor Frost died after a long battle with cancer and heart disease. Three years passed before Frost buried her ashes himself in the cemetery of the First Congregational Church in Old Bennington. Her death weighed heavily upon him as he grieved for the personal sacrifices which his pursuit of poetry had caused her to make throughout her life. It was from poetry, however, that Frost gained consolation as he lived alone on his Vermont farm. The direction and emphasis of his work was to be forever changed.

By July 1938, Kay Morrison (married and twenty-five years his junior) had become his lover and was to be his constant companion for the last twenty-five years of his life, an exercise in which her husband, Ted, cooperated. Neither could save the troubled Carol, who shot himself on 9 October 1940, a victim of family insanity

A move to Boston

In October 1938, Frost persuaded Kay Morrison to become his secretary and moved to an apartment in Boston. Later that year he purchased a farm near Ripton, Vermont, as his summer residence. In 1941 he bought his final home in

Cambridge, a short walk from Harvard University, where he had become Harvard Fellow in American Civilisation.

A Witness Tree and *Steeple Bush*

Published on 23 April 1942, *A Witness Tree* was dedicated to Kay, and the sexual imagery of its love poems is as powerful as its exploration of the emotion of love is subtle.

Frost continued to teach at Harvard until America's entry into the Second World War after the bombing of Pearl Harbor, when he moved on to Dartmouth College as Humanities Fellow, publishing *Steeple Bush* in 1947. There he remained until 1949 when he took up his last teaching post in 1949, again at Amherst.

The later years

Frost was now known as America's sage. In 1958 he was made Poetry Consultant at the Library of Congress and was a regular diner at the White House. He became in his last years America's roving literary ambassador, visiting Brazil, Israel and Moscow. He spoke at President Kennedy's inauguration.

Frost's ninth book, *In the Clearing*, was published in 1962 when he was 88 years old. He died on 29 January 1963.

3

The poet in close-up

An autobiographical poet

Frost presents events and individuals that are part of his own personal history. His characters are finely drawn with their own distinct personalities, but at the same time look beyond the circumscribed to the fate of humanity, to universal abstracts of the meaning and purpose of life in the history of humankind. The emotive abstracts so explored in the poems are developed from a careful record of personal and physical details. They define Frost's (and thus humankind's) capacity for sexual predation, selfishness, curiosity, rebellion, philosophy, vacillation, suspicion, fellowship and exclusion.

A poet of landscape

Natural worlds – in particular, the landscapes of New England – dominate Frost's work and are carefully recorded with an artist's eye for detail, colour and atmosphere and a poet's ear for sound. Explored with precision and depth and in literal and figurative imagery, their physical reality is developed into a symbolic significance.

His nature poetry is patterned by many memorable images which have a psychological as well as physical reality. These images define the hand of nature on the landscape and the forces that control the cosmos, indifferent and at times inimical to the needs of humankind.

A poet of gladness and suffering

Frost's poetry explores humankind's strongest feelings: the grief and pain and suffering and the odd moments of joy and fellowship and hope that is a universal experience. His work is a human documentary of:
* raw fear and frustration
* excitement and exhilaration
* exhaustion of the body and of the spirit

- the power and enduring nature of grief
- the dangers and cruelties of passion
- despair which threatens to overwhelm the spirit
- the attraction of suicide and of the escape which it offers from the tribulations of the world
- the joys of friendship and companionship
- the trials of marriage
- the bonds forged between those who work at simple menial tasks
- the strength of self and of simple human dignity
- the dignity of honest rural labour
- the (often unrecognised) craving of the human spirit for meaning
- the joys to be found and the pain to be experienced in the world
- the serenity of rural life
- the realities of isolation, loneliness and estrangement

A creator of myth and parable

Frost's poetry is coloured with narratives which deal with moral and spiritual relationships between humankind and the cosmos. 'Stopping by Woods on a Snowy Evening' examines, for example, the susceptibility of human consciousness to nature's welcoming of self-annihilation. 'Mending Wall' examines with parable-like simplicity that selfish self-centredness of humankind which alienates individuals from each other and feeds deep-seated suspicions. 'The Mountain' examines the motivation for heroic journeys and the universe's consciousness of the presence of humankind, and its desire to safeguard the secrets of existence from inquiry. 'The Bear' portrays the intellectual and emotional confusion which attends such inquiry.

A presenter of universal experience

Rural America provided Frost with the average people and the images by which he defines humankind's universal experience. His universal themes include:
- the power and strength of humankind's spiritual existence
- the continuity of life through birth and death and the inescapable nature of suffering
- the waste that is part of life and nature
- the power of the forces which control the cosmos, and humankind's insignificance in the universal scheme
- the capacity of endurance in the individual
- the thirst of the human spirit for meaning; the search for answers to the problems of existence

- the power of love
- the perpetuation of suspicion and mistrust
- the survival in modern humankind of the bloodlust of our primitive forebears
- the nobility that can be found in a life lived simply
- the struggle of existence
- the decay of rural culture and the changing face of mechanised civilisation
- the human capacity for aggression and hatred
- the reality of common experience
- the power of pain and the common bond of grief
- decadence, suffering and decay
- the cycle of life including the promise of birth, the rituals of adulthood and the vagaries of old age
- human mortality and the brevity of human existence
- the transience and mutability of all things – change as the essential fact of life
- the decay of personal relationships – husband to wife, friend to friend, parent to child – and the suspicion that attends our dealings with others
- the sadness and poignancy that is the essential nature of experience
- the forceful presence of death at the rim of human consciousness
- the insignificance of – yet nobility of – individual lives
- humankind's capacity for cruelty
- the power of the human ego
- the psychological and emotional consequences of the vastness of the universe
- the complexities of the human psyche

4

The poems in close-up

A Boy's Will (1913)

'Into My Own'

This poem is a poignant reconstruction of the negative feelings which drove Frost in November 1894 to walk into the dense wasteland of Dismal Swamp which extends for over forty kilometres on the Virginia – North Carolina border, in a half-hearted attempt to commit suicide. It constructs a kind of dreamland, vast and dark and dangerous in its labyrinth of snake-infested earth and seemingly endless trees.

RESEARCH BEFORE YOU READ

- Locate Dismal Swamp in an atlas of North America, and research the wildlife to be found there.
- Read Shakespeare's treatment of melancholy in Hamlet's contemplation of suicide in his soliloquy 'To be or not to be …' (Act 3 Scene 1).
- Read Shakespeare's Sonnet 116 and note Frost's allusion to the line: 'But bears it out even to the edge of doom.'
- Read Edgar Allan Poe's 'Dream-Land' – a source of Frost's poem.
- Consider your own experience of 'the blues'.
- Read John Keats' 'Ode to a Nightingale' and consider its evocation of an individual's desire to escape the troubles of existence by finding oblivion in nature.
- Consider the Slough of Despond in Bunyan's *Pilgrim's Progress*. Is not despair the greatest inhibitor of human action and the greatest destroyer of human resolve?

A CLOSER ANALYSIS

The first stanza of the poem is a statement of one of the narrator's wishes. What is implied by the fact that he seemingly has many? What is the effect of such a close association of 'wishes' with 'dark trees'? One of sadness? Profound despair? A sense of loss? Are not the simple words dense with emotion (a little like the trees?).

The trees are firm in spite of their age. How strong a sense of time is evoked by this image? They have been resistant to change and continue to be scarcely affected by the breeze. Could the same be said for the narrator?

What is the effect of the metaphor of the mask? Does it suggest trickery on nature's part, or by the force that controls the universe? Ephemerality? Is it a symbol of the unfathomable mysteries of the natural world? How does the alliteration of 'm' in line 3 contribute to the tone, meaning and atmosphere of the poem at this point? With a suggestion of disgust? A tone of disappointment? Is it too strong to suggest a sense of derision here?

The last phase of the fourth line imaginatively transports the reader to the ends of both the earth and of time. How physical and how visual is the image? How desperate is the desolation expressed by this wish? How strong the desire for oblivion, the urge to suicide which it captures? How does the sound and the length of the sound of 'away' and the rhyming of the long ominous sound of 'oom' contribute to the meaning?

The second stanza expresses a strong longing for escape – again a sense of being swallowed up by the world is captured in the long sound of 'day', the voice drifting off into silence. The speaker is 'fearless' about ever finding the open land which expresses the clearing hand of man or the highway which is the road back to that world from whence he has come. How powerfully suggestive is the metaphor of the automobile as an animal presented in the pun of 'pour'? What judgment of humanity might be contained in this animal image? What is the effect of 'pour' in the literal sense? Does it capture the slow progress of a vehicle through sand? And by doing so capture the struggle to survive in a world which largely works against humankind? How does the road image develop from the stretching distance of the first stanza?

The first line of stanza 3 consists entirely of monosyllables. Is its emotion more dramatically presented by such simplicity of diction? The road image is now a 'track' yet the highway remains in the reader's consciousness through the reminder presented in the reference to overtaking. Do the remaining lines of this stanza suggest a confidence in his loved ones following him to rescue him from the peril he is seeking, or a loss of such confidence? Is the last line not an expression of confidence in his own self-worth? Is it egotistical in the importance it ascribes to others' affection for him? Has the mood of the poem changed at this point? Is the suicidal despair replaced by a revived certainty of self-worth?

How does the last couplet explain the narrator's motives? Do they reveal a sinister desire to test those who love him by an attempted suicide? Do they change your feelings towards him? Make him appear cruel? Exploitative? Unfeeling? Self-indulgent?

How appropriate is Frost's choice of the sonnet form? Is it the right genre to express such intensity of emotion?

Poetic techniques

The poem is dominated by imagery of the earth, the landscape and roads as it evokes a (perhaps half-hearted) attempt at a last journey:

*   dark trees
*   gloom stretching to or hiding the horizon (reflecting the psychological darkness engulfing the poet)
*   the open clearings made by man
*   sandy highway
*   personal tracks through sand

How passive a landscape is it? Does the 'pour'(paw) reference change this? Note also the image of deception in the mask. How unfriendly is the universe evoked by these images? How small and insignificant is the individual in its vastness?

The simplicity of the poem's language adds to the drama of the physical and psychological landscape of the poem. It gives the poem a raw intensity and a firmness of thought. Note:

*   the whispered sounds of the first stanza – in words like 'wishes', 'trees', 'breeze', ''twere' and 'merest' and the powerful atmospheric effect of the poet's use of rhyme
*   the dramatic effect of the placement of 'fearless' at the beginning of line 7
*   the dramatic flourish of the final couplet, and the sense of confidence established by its rhyme
*   the sense of control and definiteness of resolve created by the three single statements of the first three quatrains and the monosyllabic word endings

Themes

Think about the poem's exploration of these themes:

*   the vastness of the physical landscape
*   the powerful interaction between the human psyche and the physical world – one becomes a symbol for the other

- the power of melancholy and despair and the powerful attraction of suicide to an individual beset by these emotions
- the importance and saving power of love; the human need to be loved
- the power of the mind to 'work through' the darkest thoughts
- the attraction of oblivion when set against the difficulties evoked by living
- the indifference of nature to the suffering of humankind

Universal elements

- the vast expanse of the natural world and the physical, emotional and intellectual challenges it throws out to humankind
- the attraction of death
- the struggle that is existence
- the power of love

YOUR SECOND RESPONSE

1. Assess the effectiveness of the poem's use of simple language to convey pure emotion. How does the poet's use of rhyme and sound define that emotion?
2. Discuss Frost's achievement in this poem. How finely balanced is its treatment of the external landscape of the swamp and the internal landscape of the narrator's feelings?
3. How does Frost exploit the possibilities of the sonnet form in this poem? (Consider especially the contribution made by the rhyme scheme and by each quatrain to the development of the argument. Is there a 'twist' to the poem's thesis in the final couplet?)

'A Late Walk'

This poem is an exploration of negatives, counterbalanced by the final somewhat surprising gentle thought. It is structured on Frost's favourite motif of a journey.

RESEARCH BEFORE YOU READ

Observe the evidence of time passing and of decay in the landscape around you.

YOUR FIRST RESPONSE

A CLOSER ANALYSIS

The poem begins gently with the introductory definition of the landscape into which the poet is walking: a freshly mown field. This gentleness makes the image of the second line even more surprising in its metaphorical conjuring of the horror of decapitation. How strong a word is 'aftermath'? How does it balance the strength of the idea in 'headless'? Is the image appropriate or unnecessarily exaggerated? What status does it give the elements of the natural world affected by the mowing process? What status does it give the character of the human mower?

The simile of roof thatch introduces a more homely image. Is there a suggestion of blood in the heavy dew which overlays the grasses which it describes? Or does the image of the second line not linger in our imaginations sufficiently? Is the effect of the rhyme of the second and fourth lines to revive the horror of it?

What lesson about nature's attitude to humankind is implied in the behaviour of the newly mown grass as it blocks the wanderer's path? Indifference? Malicious obstruction of human progress?

The second stanza describes the state of the garden reached by the path. How effective are the adjectives used in this stanza? What is their cumulative message? That nature is cruel? That all life suffers at its hand? The onomatopoeic 'whir' of the birds describes the sound of their flight effectively. What kind of sound is it? Sad? Echoing? Energetic? Ominous? How does the alliterative use of 'w' compound the sadness of this stanza and dramatise the semantic effect of individual words? Caught up in the last line, does this repeated 'w' sound suggest the physicality of sadness as well as its emotional reality? How does the falling intonation and the steady rhythm of the final line of the second stanza contribute to the sadness of its tone and to its depiction of atmosphere?

The third stanza begins with an image of isolation – a solitary tree beside a bare wall. How does the bareness of the wall contribute to the evocation of sad solitude in this line? The sense of loneliness and of vulnerability is compounded by the image of the leaf. What additional emotional and physical darkness is given to the poem by the poet's choice of verb and the verb's immediate juxtaposition with the adjective 'brown'? The hint of a painful relinquishment of life? Is this why the next line begins with its strongest – and most disturbing – adjective? The speaker assist the leaf's demise by the power and undoubted negativity of his own thought. The leaf's final descent is gently captured by the metrical effect of the two middle words of the last line of the third stanza. Do you appreciate the linguistic subtlety here? Does it create a sense of reverence? Of respect? Of mournful quietness?

The fourth and final stanza marks the end of the speaker's perambulation – and perhaps, too, defines its purpose in his harvesting of the last aster flower, an act which aligns him with the beheading mowers of the first stanza. Does this gesture of love fully counterbalance the poem's concentration on dying nature? Does its acknowledgment of the human partnership counter the solitary motifs which dominate the imaginative landscape of the poem and climax in the singular flower itself? Or does it, in its gentleness, merely act as a final defining counterpoint to the dark truths about life explored in the poem? Or does the reality of the act catch up too strongly the grim imagery of the first stanza?

Poetic techniques

The poem is dominated by images of solitariness, sadness and dying. Each stanza depicts a death – the first a harvesting of a whole field; the second a bed of dead weeds; the third a harvesting (even by the poet's own thought) of a leaf and the fourth the poet's harvesting of the final aster in that brave flower's final defeat.

The placement of words (check out the first words/phrases of lines 3, 9, 10 and 13) and the isolation of the particular phrase of line 2 add to the poem's dramatic sense. The use of alliteration, onomatopoeia and rhyme contributes a further mournful resonance.

The dominance of monosyllabic words contributes to the poem's exploration of its theme of isolation – in particular of the 'I'.

The motif of the journey dominates the poem – the speaker's journey, but also the journey of all living things to death.

Themes

Think about these thematic possibilities:

*   isolation of individual lives (the speaker's and each tree, leaf and flower) in nature
*   the struggle that each living creature has for existence and the inevitability of defeat and of death
*   humankind's mark on the landscape as a destroyer
*   the beauty and ugliness that is to be found in nature
*   the power and beauty of love and its particular value in the grimness that characterises the cosmos
*   the vastness of the cosmos and its vast indifference to the sufferings of all living things

Universal elements

The poem explores the inevitability and reality of death in the landscape, the transience of all things in nature and the value of love and of beauty in the midst of the annihilating forces which control the universe.

YOUR SECOND RESPONSE

1. Analyse the poetic techniques employed by Frost to give universal signifi-
    cance to a garden walk.
2. What insights does this poem provide into Frost's a poetic themes and his
    understanding of humankind's relationship with the cosmos?

'Stars'

In this poem, Frost re-expresses Thomas Hardy's philosophy that the universe is
at best indifferent to the sufferings of humankind, and at worst actively malicious.
From Hardy, too, he has taken the symbol of distant stars as representative of the
smallness of man and woman in the enormous space of the cosmos driven by
forces which are far beyond the comprehension and the concern of humankind.

RESEARCH BEFORE YOU READ

*   Research the story of Minerva, the goddess of wisdom.
*   Read Thomas Hardy's depiction of a cold universe in his description of the skies
    which oversee the sufferings of his characters Tess of the D'Urbervilles and the
    Mayor of Casterbridge.
*   Read Coleridge's poem 'Christabel' and note how the stars in that poem's land-
    scape are associated with the malevolence of the main character.

YOUR FIRST RESPONSE

A CLOSER ANALYSIS

The poem begins with a sense of wonder on the speaker's part at the seeming
infiniteness of the stars which shine above another infinity – the tumultuous
snow. How would you characterise the metaphors of this first stanza? Strongly
visual? Tactile? Animated? Symbolic statements of the annihilating power of
nature? Note the onomatopoeic breathlessness of the imagery of the winds and
the contribution to the rhythmic and aural effect of the descriptive phrases made
by the alliteration of 'w' and the assonance of 'ow' and 'l'. This landscape is dan-
gerously alive – yet without human presence – a product of elemental forces.

   The simile of the second stanza attributes an active malevolence to these
elements as they hasten us to our graves. Human life is lived with little confidence. All travel is a weary path to oblivion. How does the rhythm of 'few
faltering' capture this idea? By a lightness and quickness of sound (created by the

combination of the alliteration of 'f' with the trisyllabic word 'faltering') which is in stark contrast to the numbing heaviness of the sound and effect of 'snow'?

The last line of the second stanza marks the end of the wintry night and the coming of dawn which reveals only the obliteration of the landscape – even the graveyards.

The third stanza expresses the speaker's philosophical rationale of the events of the evening. Minerva – the goddess of wisdom, and the controlling power of this white universe – is sightless, and therefore indifferent to the operation of the elements of her world. How do the metaphors of lines 10 and 11 bring together the elements of earth, water and wind which are the dominant forces of the cosmos that she rules? How strongly is the sense of death defined in the description of her eyes? Does the reference to white marble retrospectively add further resonance to the poem's description of graves?

Poetic techniques

The poem is dominated by the image of the stars – powerful symbols of the indifference of the universe to the sufferings of humankind and by imagery of obliteration.

In the centre (the literal centre) of the poem falters humankind – its steps hesitant and its being soon obliterated by the negative forces of the universe symbolised in the bitter winds and the cold snow of winter.

The poet makes effective use of alliteration and assonance to define his ideas. Also note the particular effect of the two trisyllabic words – the first to suggest infinite numbers, the second to suggest struggle and powerlessness.

Themes

Think about these thematic possibilities:
• the coldness and vastness of the universe
• the insignificance of humankind in the cosmos
• the indifference of the universal mind to human life and suffering
• the power of death

Universal elements

The poem imbues a winter landscape with the symbols of nature's indifference to and inevitable destruction of humankind.

YOUR SECOND RESPONSE

1. Is the ultimate effect and meaning of 'Stars' derived from its symbolism?

2. Is 'Stars' Frost's statement about the nature of existence? Is there any beauty in the universe of the poem? Can the forces of destruction have their own beauty?

'Mowing'

'Mowing' is a pastoral poem, an exploration of the place of humankind in nature as part of its inevitable cycle of birth and death. As such it continues a classical tradition that extends from Theocritus, a Greek poet of the third century BC who wrote poems about the life of Sicilian shepherds, and from Virgil who, in Latin, transformed the Greek model into a conventional poem expressing the simplicity and peace of country folk in idealised natural settings.

The poem is a celebration of the joy of both rural and poetic labour and the meaning to existence which both bring. It is also a celebration of the sound of the scythe and the sound of the poet's voice as an expression of life.

RESEARCH BEFORE YOU READ

*   Read Andrew Marvell's 'The Mower Against Gardens' and William Wordsworth's 'The Solitary Reaper'. Note Frost's allusions to lines in these poems.
*   Research and note the resonances in this poem of the song 'Fear No More the Heat of the Sun' from Shakespeare's *Cymbeline*.
*   Research the medieval allegorical figure of the Grim Reaper.
*   Research the symbolism of the snake in Christian mythology.

YOUR FIRST RESPONSE

A CLOSER ANALYSIS

The poem opens with an acknowledgment of the voice of the scythe which cuts its path into the silence of the landscape. How effective is the personification and the onomatopoeia in giving life to this voice? The sound carries a secret message, the meaning of which the poet can only guess at: a fact about the sun's heat, or about the silence itself. What is achieved by the repetition of 'something' here? A dramatisation of the essential and ultimately unfathomable mysteries of the universe? A suggestion of something too profound – or too shocking – to be uttered?

Its message was not one of easy hours or easy wealth; these things pale into insignificance against the meaning of this (and every) harvest.

How do the adjectives contribute to the poem's meaning? What is so special about 'earnest love'? Its commitment? Its sincerity? The concentration of will it demands? Why are the spikes of the flowers so weak tipped? Is it that their energy is sapped by the demands of living? By the necessary competition with the surrounding grasses?

What is achieved by the juxtaposition of the pale orchises with the bright green snake? Does this symbolise the triumph of evil over good?

Is there something very significant in the fact that the man frightens the snake? Is this image more than a statement of the potential for cruelty in human power? Does it imply a greater potential for evil in humankind than in the snake (Satan or the vile force of the universe)?

Is the very joy of the message in the fact that it remains indecipherable and exists merely as a companionable voice to the lonely mower?

Poetic techniques

This poem is dominated by strong images: of man in the landscape, of his fellow creature the snake, both vibrant expressions of the life force. The snake takes on an almost mythical quality as the snake in a reincarnation of the Garden of Eden. Does its presence suggest evil or is it merely an acknowledgment that this is a corrupt universe, that human toil is directly related to sinfulness? Or has Frost pared from the snake its Christian connotations to make it symbolic of the vibrancy of life?

The sound of the blade cutting hay mirrors the whisper of a human voice – and creates in its repeated phrases the dialogue of an imaginary companion to both the snake and the man.

Is the speaker armed with his scythe a symbolic image of the Grim Reaper figure of medieval cosmology?

Themes

Think about the following thematic possibilities:
* the worth of honest rural toil
* the beauty of life
* the natural cycle of life and death of which humankind is a part and in which it takes part

Universal elements

The poem explores the value of human toil in close association with the earth and its creatures. In celebrating life, it also, however, provides a symbolic representation of the Grim Reaper (Death) which harvests all life. Perhaps this is the elusive message contained in the mysterious dialogue which is created by the sound of the scythe.

YOUR SECOND RESPONSE

1. Analyse Frost's achievement within the sonnet genre in this poem.
2. Examine the philosophical considerations of the poem. Is the speaker's naivety about the message heavily ironic in that it is his ignorance of the truth of its message which allows him his moments of happiness in his toil?

'The Tuft of Flowers'

The poem recounts a journey by the speaker to discover the mysterious figure who has mown the grass before dawn and the lesson he draws from this experience. It is another of Frost's pastoral poems and repeats a favourite image of the mower as well as a favourite line from 'Mowing'.

RESEARCH BEFORE YOU READ

Explore the pastoral poems previously listed for 'Mowing'. You may like to extend your research to Spenser's 'Shepherd's Calendar' (1579), Sir Philip Sidney's 'Arcadia', Marlowe's 'The Passionate Shepherd to His Love' and Shakespeare's *As You Like It* which is based on a pastoral romance by Thomas Lodge, and Alexander Pope's 'Pastorals' (1709).

YOUR FIRST RESPONSE

A CLOSER ANALYSIS

The dramatic setting of the poem is created in the first couplet. Is there beauty in this first image? Serenity? A sense of timelessness?

The second image is tougher. It records the desolation left by the early mower. The image of the blade challenges the simple innocence of the introduction.

The third couplet expands the details of the scene – it adds visual, auditory and tactile depth. What is the impact of the reference to the 'whetstone'? The introduction of utilitarianism? A reminder of the physicality of rural labour? An antidote to cloying romanticism?

The early labourer is not to be found. The speaker, like the one before him, is all alone – a fact that is rationalised as the 'way of things', the reality of every individual's existence. What is the effect of the internalised conversation? The establishment of an introspective melancholy?

Nature answers the sad thought of the speaker even as it is given words. The butterfly surprises him in the suddenness and noiselessness of its appearance. Its confusion is echoed in the alliterative use of 'w', the second repetition of the sound caught up in the middle of 'bewildered', and in the stumbling rhythm created by the alliteration of 'b'.

The butterfly is a fellow searcher, seeking alas, that which is now lost, swallowed by time and the mower's scythe. What dramatic emphasis is given to the creature's motivation by the selection of the first words of this seventh couplet – and by their alliteration?

The speaker observes the sad discovery to which the butterfly's journey leads, the desperation attending the search captured in the circularity of sound in the first line of this couplet. What reality is given to the dying flower by the speaker's use of the trisyllabic 'withering'? Is the single flower's death given greater poignancy by the fact that its dying is still in process?

The ninth couplet states simply a perfectly magical moment – the butterfly's return to the speaker after its reconnaissance of the landscape. What is the meaning of its action? An acknowledgment of the companionship of all things? That the speaker and the creature are the two sole living beings in their landscape? How confident is the butterfly of its security in approaching the speaker? What else is suggested by its tremulousness? The creature's own fragility? Its beautiful delicacy? Its understanding of the vulnerabilities and dangers faced by any living being? Is the vastness of the landscape established in the first line of this couplet a contributing factor to its fearfulness?

The speaker ponders the significance of the event but, finding the questions raised by it unfathomable, goes to turn away. Perhaps to bury his anxiety in the ritual of labour?

The butterfly's flight path is to another expression of life in the landscape – the tall tuft of flowers beside a brook. The dignity of the flowers is captured in the confident rhythmical firmness of the words selected to describe them. How does the alliterative use of 't' contribute to the effect?

The flowers' height is reiterated in the metaphor of the twelfth couplet. The surmise of their survival is conveyed in the repetition of 'scythe', the destroyer of all their kind who out of vagary or sympathy or even, perhaps, admiration, had chosen to spare them. What kind of energy is captured in the choice of the adjective 'leaping'? Aggressive? Vital? Does the reed-choked brook have its own secrets?

The reason for the survival of the tuft of flowers is to be found in the pre-dawn mower's appreciation of their beauty in the beauty of the morning. How rare – and therefore how much more valuable – is this expression by Frost of a moment of sheer joy. How does the rhyme of 'him' and 'brim' concentrate the reaper's feeling of happy plenitude?

The speaker interprets the tuft of flowers as a message from the dawn. What does his use of the word 'lit' contribute to the emphasis of the poem at this point on the greater understanding of existence to be gained by close association with nature?

The message is aurally defined in the sixteenth couplet. The bird song intrudes on the speaker's consciousness at the same time as the sound of the early mower's scythe intrudes on the ear of his imagination. How effective is the rhythmical effect of the use of 'wakening' and 'whispering' and their connection semantically as well as metrically with the alliterative use of 'w'? Is each image in this couplet a statement of the vitality and energy of life?

The speaker feels a link to the early mower. On what is this connection based? Merely their common humanity? Their bond with the earth? Their joint appreciation of natural beauty? What is the value of the feeling? A sense of human society? A solution to the agony of loneliness?

What is achieved by the speaker's repeated reference to the mower as his companion? Is there a sense of the surreal or paranormal in the spiritual and emotional contact between the two? How strongly visual – and symbolic – is the image? Is it a physical statement of the commonality of experience (and fears and need for companionship) shared by all humankind? How comforting is the repeated sound of the rhyme?

The 'brotherly' speech is an imagined dialogue – but of real significance to the speaker. Why? What is its meaning? How does it contribute to the universality of the speaker's singular experience in the light of this early morning?

Poetic techniques

The poem consists of twenty rhyming couplets and develops its thesis about human existence by the steady enlightenment of the speaker in the early morning light as he contemplates the images that are revealed by the dawn. The poem does not depart from the rhythms of natural speech but achieves a serenity as well as a dramatic emphasis through its use of rhyme and metre. After all, in the quietness of early morning do not all sounds take on a special significance?

The images are selective and sensual: all senses are awakened in the taste, touch and smell of the dew, in the breeze's caress; in the smell of new-mown grass; in the sound and delicacy of the butterfly's wing; in the sound of the awakening birds and in the visual and tactile beauty of the spike of flowers; in the sound of the brook and of the scythe 'whispering to ground' in the heat of the noon sun and the coolness and colour of the shade.

Themes

Think about the following thematic possibilities:

- the bond between all living things (the speaker and the butterfly; the butterfly and the tuft of flowers; the mower and the tuft of flowers; the speaker and the mower; the mower and the birds)
- the power of beauty
- the nature and power of love
- the need of humankind for society
- the pangs of loneliness
- the vulnerabilities and vagaries of existence – the role of chance
- the fragility and brevity of life
- the vastness of nature
- the presence of the power of all the elements – earth, water, fire (the heat of the sun) and wind (air)

Universal elements

The landscape is rural countryside which is a pastoral symbol of idyllic nature in which a man can employ himself in honest labour and at the same time gain wisdom from close association with the earth and the elements which mould it.

YOUR SECOND RESPONSE

1. Can this poem be dismissed as merely an exercise in an old-fashioned poetic (pastoral) form or does it, in its simplicity, provide profound insight into the meaning of existence?
2. Analyse the contribution of the imagery of 'The Tuft of Flowers' to its meaning.
3. Is this one of Frost's more positive poems in its choice of subject matter and theme?

North of Boston (1914)

'Mending Wall'

At lease some of the inspiration for this poem came from Frost's observation of an advertisement on a picket fence promoting fencing by proclaiming that 'Good fences make good neighbours'. Some also came from Christ's prophecy set out in St Matthew's Gospel about the future destruction– stone by stone – of Herod's temple to false values. The rest came from Frost's belief in the impossibility of defining absolutely the boundaries between good and evil or any two abstract opposing propositions.

RESEARCH BEFORE YOU READ

- Read St Matthew's Gospel 24:2.
- Read Byron's poem 'She Walks in Beauty' and note Frost's allusion to its lines: 'She walks in beauty, like the night ...'

YOUR FIRST RESPONSE

A CLOSER ANALYSIS

The very first word of the poem establishes the sense of that which colours its entire atmosphere. How powerful is the effect of the capitalisation of 'Something'? Do we forget that the capital first letter could merely be a matter of the word being the first uttered in the poem? Does 'love' take on a special significance when placed in a line of such basic vocabulary? Is the poet not paring down the complexities of existence in this poem in order to reach a fundamental core of meaning?

Does line 1 not leave us with a sense of a powerful unknown force operating in the cosmos?

What are the natural elements captured in the phrase 'frozen-ground-swell'? Earth? Cold? Water/ice? What tensions are captured in this description – especially in the semantic contrast between the first and third word? What drama is captured by the juxtaposition of three quite ordinary words? What events are anticipated here?

The third line leads on to the resolution of the tension established in the second – again a simple word, 'spills', takes on an extraordinary power. Mountains – or at least the elements of man-made mountains – the boulders of the wall are moved and tumble to the earth under the sun. What is the significance of the reference to the sun here? Does it assign an intensity to the moment of spillage? Does it serve as a reminder of the vast canopy of the universe under which this small but powerfully meaningful event occurs? Does it suggest nature's indifference to it all?

Note how the enjambment (run on) of line 2 into line 3 reflects in the uninterrupted flow of the metrical line the gathering of the force which eventually spills the boulders.

What is achieved by the final image of the fourth line? Does it merely establish a visual epilogue to the process which has just been recounted? Is it unnecessarily ugly? Is the plurality of the gaps created symptomatic of the power of the 'force'? Is the image powerfully symbolic of its destructive capacity? Is the fact that this destructive seemingly omnipotent force is frost – a deliberate

implied pun by the poet on his own name? Is there a hidden message here as some critics have suggested? An expression of the poet's ego perhaps? Or a pose deliberately and teasingly adopted by the poet? A riddle?

Having commenced in the elemental and spiritual arena, Frost moves to the more human world of hunters in the next phase of the poem. The sense of mystery continues to be sustained, however, in the echo of the 'something' of the first line in 'thing.' The hunters are a race apart from the speaker – for it is the speaker who comes after them to repair the damage they do in the service of their bloodlust. Is it their motivation, the origin of their destructive desires, which is their mystery? Is it their cruelty which aligns them with that other unknown force?

How powerful is the image of the 'yelping dogs' (egged on by hunters) hunting a lone rabbit? Is this not yet another dramatic enactment of one of Frost's main themes – the vulnerability, harshness and brevity of existence of all living things? The image is visual and auditory. Is it also olfactory? Is there a 'smell of blood' about it? Is it not a hunger for the prey's blood which aligns man and dog in hunting? Is the boundary between man and dog therefore so easily drawn? How does the progressive aspect of the adjective 'yelping' contribute to the energy of the scene? Does it add a sense of time to the episode – reminding the reader that the discovery and killing of the rabbit demands sustained commitment from both the dogs and their master? A sustained joint emotive commitment to destruction of a fellow living creature?

The hunting image becomes, however, but a dramatic aside to the main concern of the poem – a more earthly consideration of an expression of that force which is responsible for the unexplained gaps which seasonally and mysteriously appear in the wall and await discovery in the spring with all the patience of the cosmos.

Their discovery causes the speaker to approach his neighbour so that they can perform their springtime ritual repair. It is a ritual which has its own paradox – it causes two neighbours to cooperate so that the wall which separates them can be sustained. It divides even their energies at this moment as they keep the wall between them as they walk its line. The words which describe the incident are all the more dramatic for their monosyllabic simplicity. They define the ritual in strong symbolic terms – a statement of humankind's determination to hang on to all that divides it. Does the simplicity of the language and the ritualistic nature of the description create a visual parable? Imbue the men's behaviour with a significance akin to one of Christ's parables? Is there an echo of the parables of Christ in the reference to the 'loaves'?

The variety of the boulders is a symbolic statement of the variety of even passive nature. Yet that variety is itself a challenge as the different shapes require different manoeuvres in order for them to be placed. What is the effect of the speaker's reference to 'spell' here? What is the point of the speaker's utterance? A good-hearted recognition of the pointlessness of the whole exercise?

Dealing with the stones and reconstructing the wall roughens the neighbours' hands. Does not humankind's involvement in life mark the physical (and emotional and psychological) being?

And what, then, in the end is created out of the exertion of each? Nothing that will endure. The ephemeral nature of all humankind's constructions is summed up in the image the speaker ascribes to his and his neighbour's efforts. It is, after all, just a game.

What is the full effect of the game metaphor? Does it not reproduce – reduced to the utmost simplicity – the nature of all human confrontations? Is not war a 'game' between two sides?

The game is, after all, of little point (as war and other conflict is of little point). The differences between the two define them but do not in essence place them in conflict. Their activities are after all complementary – different but of the same kind. Does not Frost sum up in this simple dramatic image his belief that all conflicting ideas are reducible in the end to the same basic premises?

The speaker's neighbour refuses to be convinced (as the speaker is) of the fact that the wall is unnecessary. His answer is a platitude – unthinkingly but confidently uttered. What is it that drives him to say this? Thoughtlessness? An innate suspicion of everyone else? Greed? Ego? A desire for separateness? A sense of fear that in companionship he might lose his own identity?

Egged on by spring – by his own companionship with nature – the speaker wonders if he could challenge his neighbour's complacent acceptance of the alienating cliche. He rehearses his statement, his rationalisation of his questioning of the efficacy of walls. Are his words Frost's challenge to all of us who like, repair and build walls to think about our reasons for doing so? What effect is achieved by the repetition of the first line?

How is the original mystery of this line increased by the additional reference to elves? Does capitalisation of 'Elves' contribute to its effectiveness? Why is it 'not elves exactly'? Is there no explanation in the realms of magic for the unknown force? Does its power belong to a more omnipotent realm?

Why does the speaker prefer that his neighbour should come to the same conclusion about the lack of meaning in walls himself? Is it that the understanding and imagination which cause us to revise our bigotry and to abandon our misguided thoughts are only self-discoverable rather than teachable?

The final image of the poem transports us back to the beginnings of humanity and of communal living. It defines the consequence and ultimate meaning of any neighbour's ennobling of walls. The darkness of the trees through which the neighbour moves is symbolic of the more significant darkness in which he lives his life. Is this other darkness moral? Spiritual? Psychological? Intellectual? Emotional? All of these?

What is it that keeps the neighbour in this darkness? Habit? A blind adherence to the tenets of his father? An unthinking acceptance of the standards of his community? Farming practice? What final comment is made on his position by his repetition of his father's saying? Is the saying not the cliche in which humankind hides distrustful self-seeking and elitism?

Poetic techniques

The language of the poem is strongly and simply colloquial – its moments of dialogue dramatically punctuate the speaker's narration of the ritual of alienation.

The poem's imagery is all the more dramatic and powerful in its effect because of its simplicity. The atmosphere is dominated by a sense of magic and of mystery. Note the use of capitalisation. Also note:

- the effective sense of mystery captured in the repetition of key words and phrases
- the density and tension captured in the epithet of line 2
- the parable-like simplicity of the speaker's dialogue
- the effective use of enjambment to suggest a relentless process

The wall is a powerful symbol of all the walls – physical, emotional, intellectual, religious, psychological, political, ethical – which individuals construct to keep others at bay.

Themes

Consider the following thematic possibilities:

- our readiness to ascribe to the workings of the supernatural all that is not understandable
- the power of suspicion and its impediment to greater understanding between human beings
- the alienation/isolation of the individual
- humankind's mistrust of those who are different
- the pointless rituals of human lives
- the unnecessary boundaries which divide humankind
- the survival in modern humankind of primitive bloodlust
- the ephemeral nature of our achievements
- the powerlessness of humankind against the greater forces of the universe
- the smallness of humankind in the cosmos
- the tenacity with which most of us protect our property and our individuality

Universal elements

The poem explores the simple ritual of two neighbours' maintenance of a wall constructed by past generations as a metaphor for the human persistence in maintaining barriers between individuals which celebrate the superficial differences between them just as they ignore the intrinsic commonality of their experience.

The poem also explores the power of ancient suspicions as well as the reason for their origin – the innate bloodlust and cruelty of humankind.

YOUR SECOND RESPONSE

1. What insight does 'Mending Wall' provide into the efficacy of the proposition, 'Good fences make good neighbours'? How effectively does it present its argument?
2. Does 'Mending Wall' suggest a more positive future for humankind?
3. Is 'Mending Wall' a parable?

'The Death of the Hired Man'

Three very different characters reveal themselves through dialogue in 'Death of the Hired Man', a poem which explores the different capacities of the man and his wife for human sympathy and empathy and the inherent right of even the poorest man for respect, particularly at the moment of his death. In the poverty and simplicity of its setting the poem creates a dramatic situation and atmosphere that is reminiscent of a Thomas Hardy cottage, a haven from the trials and tribulations which characterise Everyman's life journey.

RESEARCH BEFORE YOU READ

- Read Thomas Hardy's 'The Darkling Thrush'.
- Research details of the rural worker's cottage of the late 19th and early 20th century.
- Read *Waiting for Godot* by Samuel Beckett, and note the playwright's creation of suspense.
- Read George Eliot's *Silas Marner*. Note this author's exploration of the isolation of an old man.

YOUR FIRST RESPONSE

A CLOSER ANALYSIS

The poem begins strongly with its dramatic alliteration of 'm'. What resonances are created by this technique? A reminder of the simple beginnings of fairytales?

A variation on 'Once upon a time'? A subtle suggestion of the Mary of the Nativity? Of innocent simplicity? Is the atmosphere created by the image of a woman alone at night, her thoughts focused on the lamp's flame, romantic? Sinister? Expectant? Anxious? Fearful? One of time standing still?

The alliteration of the first line is parallelled by the alliteration of line 2. What effect does the placement of 'Waiting' (and its consequent capitalisation) have on the idea presented? Is Frost deliberately overdramatising the situation in his phrase's echo of the Beckett play *Waiting for Godot*? Is the effect an enlarging of the character of Warren?

From the suspension of time created in the first line and a half, the poem gathers pace in the narrator's use of enjambment as the lines follow the movement of Mary − on tiptoe − to the door to greet her husband with her short message. What expectation is created of his response to her missive? Surprise? Anger? Neutrality? Joy? Has Mary's message been delivered as a warning? Or as a piece of excited − even breathless − news? Or both? Does Silas's name carry its own resonance as to its bearer's age? Or attitude?

Mary follows the delivery of her message with a series of actions: pushing Warren outside with her, shutting the door behind them and drawing him down to sit beside her on the step. How would you describe these actions and the mood created by them? Confiding? Secretive? Cautious? Domestically familiar? Fearful? Trusting? Loving?

Warren protests Mary's implication that he was ever less than kind to Silas, but is adamant that he will not have him back. The reason? Silas's desertion of Warren last haying time − and his virtual uselessness. Note the drama of Warren's simple protests on this account. How does the alliteration of 'h' and the choice of the term 'harbor' contribute to the sense of heightened emotion at this point. What are the connotations of 'harbor'? Does it suggest the desperation of Silas? His need for friends at this time?

Warren's continued review of their last encounter defines Silas's motivation and character. How is Silas defined? As a layabout? An old man hanging onto a vestige of dignity? A man without pride? A man with too much pride? A manipulator? An auctioneer of what skills and energies he has remaining?

Mary interrupts in the interests of the privacy of their conversation. Is she also concerned to save Silas's feelings should he overhear them?

Warren is unmoved − Silas must hear the truth of his feelings sooner rather than later. Warren's personal reality is defined by his idiom, as much as Mary's is by her sentiment. The details he conveys are disturbing. Note the accumulative effect of words such as 'huddled', 'miserable' and 'frightening'. What image does she portray of Silas? An isolated human being abandoned by all the rest of humankind? An animal seeking shelter? Childlike? An exhausted being?

What is it that motivates Warren's next inquiry about where Silas had been? Curiosity? Compassion? Sentiment? Sympathy? Empathy?

In reply, Mary recounts her unsuccessful efforts to get him to smoke and to talk of his travels. Silas's tiredness is emphasised in her information that she had to drag him inside the house and was unsuccessful in eliciting any conversation from him. Given the observations of Warren in ll.19–21, is Silas's refusal to smoke despite Mary's encouragement an ominous detail? Does it suggest that Silas is ill as well as exhausted?

Unmoved, Warren continues his interrogation, anxious to know whether or not Silas intends to work for him. Are his concerns ironic given Silas's condition? Mary confesses that their visitor did in fact say that he had come to 'ditch the meadow' – and to clear the upper pasture – but she offers an explanation for Silas's expressed motive in returning: even this man must preserve his sense of self-respect. The other details she conveys of Silas's dialogue are deeply disturbing. What earlier impressions of Silas do they reinforce? How do they extend the poem's portrait of him? By the suggestion of a brain addled by fatigue or age? Of decrepit senility? Of a mind returning in desperation to memories of vigour and focus?

What do Mary's observations about Silas's relationship with Harold Wilson convey about both characters? Irascibility on Silas's part? Youthful argumentativeness on Wilson's? The common testing of both by the 'blazing sun' and the physical demands of haymaking? A brotherhood forged by the rigours of toil? What is the meaning of the visual image conveyed of the old and the young man toiling together? Does Frost capture in one moment the cycle of life, the inevitability of youth's degeneration into old age? Is there a message about the collapse of farm life conveyed in Wilson's pursuit of a teaching career? An echo of the conflicts of lifestyle between teacher and farmer in Frost's own life?

Warren's response is a remembered avoidance of the tussles between the young and the old man. Note the colloquial farmer's idiom in which he expresses this. Is not the phrase 'keep well out of earshot' the utterance of a pragmatic earthy man?

Mary ponders the lingering in Silas's mind of his altercations with Wilson. Is there a pathos in the old man's attempts, seasons after they occurred, to invent arguments to counter the college boy's assurance? Is this an enactment of the universal conflict between the generations? The tension created by arrogant youth's testing of mature (though unschooled) experience? Is Frost's self-consciousness about his failure to complete his formal college education finding expression here? Is Frost comforted by Mary's sympathy? Does he seek it vicariously for himself?

What extra dramatic effect is gained by the placement of Mary's 'I sympathise' at the beginning of its poetic line and its full end stopping? What is the

bond she feels she shares with Silas? The self-consciousness of the underdog? Slow-wittedness? Is she in awe of Harold Wilson's aptitude for Latin? Is the simile she quotes from Harold comparing his study of Latin to the study of the violin an intrusion of Frost's own joy in that classical language. Does Frost identify with Harold here?

Silas's regret that he failed to make Harold believe that a man could divine water with the aid of hazel prong exemplifies the division Frost felt characterised the education of humankind – between the scholar who relies on book learning and the man of the land who relies on his knowledge of nature. Is there a valuation of the relative worth of both kinds of learning in the fact that it is building a load of hay which concludes this part of Mary's dialogue?

Warren's reply explains the huge significance to Silas of building a hay load. It is the one thing he does well. What is the message here? That everyone has one particular and special talent? That self-respect and pride can be built on simple things? That they must be built on simple things for simple rural folk? In what tone is Warren's description of Silas's special expertise narrated? Respectful? Admiring? Charitable? Generous spirited? Is Silas ennobled by Warren's account?

Silas's tagging and numbering of each bundle attests to a once agile and ordered mind. What is the effect of the contrast established between his mental capacity as a haymaker and his mental confusion in the present of the poem?

What is the effect of the simile comparing Silas's bunches of hay with birds' nests? Do both the hay bunches and birds' nests attest to the skill and intuition of their builders? Is Silas's knowledge of natural things elevated by the comparison? Is the image a recognition of his knowledge of nature and of his special part in it?

What commonsense was displayed by Silas in his haymaking? What physical strains did he avoid that a less knowledgeable and experienced man might have subjected himself to?

Why does Silas want to teach Harold Wilson the niceties of bundling hay? Is it an urge on Silas's part to convey useful life skills to the young man which his college skills will not provide him? Is it also the desire of the older generation to hand on traditions? (Compare 'Mending Wall'.) Is rural decay the social outcome of the failure of the experienced workers to do just this?

How strong a feeling is conveyed in the phrase 'the fool of books'. Is it all the more effective because of its simplicity and brevity?

Is Warren's conclusion (that Silas has nothing to look back to with pride or forward to with hope) correct? Is Warren's lack of perception and understanding of Silas's special gift – which ironically he has just described – illustrated at this point? What dramatic effect is created by the syntactic (grammatical) juxtaposition of 'forward' and 'backward'? Is there a prayer-like ending – a dreadful sense of finality – in the line 'So now and never any different.'

The passing of time as husband and wife converse is beautifully captured in the next image of the moon. What is the impact of the choice and positioning of 'dragging'? How strongly visual is the image? Is it also tactile even before the image of the light 'poured' into Mary's lap? What is the effect of 'softly'? Of Mary's humble gesture of spreading her apron to receive the gift of the cosmos? Why is Mary so especially chosen to receive the gift of light? Assess the beauty and tenderness of the next lines of the poem as Mary stretches out her hand to receive the moon's gift. Is she a Madonna figure here? A woman in touch with the rare gentleness of existence? Is the fact that the image is derivative significant? Or has Frost taken an idea and made it his own? Is the reference to 'harp' and its suggestion of angels and of heaven significant? In retrospect, does it suggest the passing of Silas's spirit?

Does the harp simile catch up the resonance established by the earlier violin simile? Is Mary in her innate kindness of spirit a player of the joys of the universe? In touch with the harmony which sometimes characterises it? Is this harmony emphasised by the cooperation of dew and light working together to produce the effect? Is the image a recognition of her intrinsic goodness? How spiritual is the tone and atmosphere created by it? How effective an overture is it to Mary's tender pronouncement that Silas has come home to die?

Warren's reply this time is a gentle mockery of her use of the word 'Home'. Does the adverb of this line save him from callousness? How powerful is the simple word 'Home', being the sum total of his immediate response and positioned as it is at the beginning of the line?

Mary is more expansive. Her comparison of Silas with the exhausted hound which also sought them out recalls Silas's position beside the barn door – and reminds us of the pathos of his situation. How is the tone and import of Warren's definition of home in reply to be described? Gruff? Resigned? Pragmatic? Cold? Matter of fact? What is the tone of Mary's juxtaposed reshaping of his words. Conciliatory? Gentle? Emphasising a sense of human duty and responsibility rather than reluctant resignation to the fact of Silas's coming?

Warren's gesture of picking up and breaking the little stick suggests his embarrassment at the miserliness of his spirit, at his lack of charity. Has Mary caused him to reconsider the situation? To evaluate his own motives? Or is he creating space in time and place to enable him to more confidently ask his next question about the relative claim Silas has upon them as opposed to his own brother? Is his confidence that Silas could and should walk the extra thirteen miles to his brother's house cruel? Does it demonstrate a lack of consideration or acceptance by him of the details of Silas's exhaustion already provided by Mary?

What is the effect of the use and placement of the term 'Somebody'? Is the brother's capacity for humanity criticised by implication? For snobbery? For self-aggrandisement?

Mary takes on the responsibility of procuring the involvement and assistance of Silas's brother 'if there is need.' Does her observation about the brother's appearances augur well for such an enterprise? Why does she raise the issue of Silas's pride in his brother? Why would Silas hesitate to claim kin? Suspicion or mistrust of his brother's education? An inability to communicate with a man who has lost touch with the earth? Does not Mary's explanation suggest pride? Is it a pride she accepts – even endorses? Should Silas be 'made ashamed to please his brother'?

Warren is at last sympathetic with the plight of the old man. How does his use of the diminutive 'Si' emphasise his sympathy?

Mary pleads with Warren to see what he can do. Her heart is hurt by his decrepitude. Note the poignant effect of the alliterative 'h' of her simple mono-syllabic words. Is not her sincerity emphasised by the poetic technique here?

Warren clings to memories of Silas's toughness, but Mary will have none of it. Her last plea is for the preservation of Silas's dignity. Her mind and imagination will wander skyward as she waits. Is the image of the 'small sailing cloud' romantic? Ominous? Both? Is the atmosphere created one of foreboding? Is the single cloud carried aloft, passing into the ether, symbolic of Silas's soul? Is the drama of the next isolated line 'It hit the moon' an echo of the drama being played out inside the house? Is the next image surreal? Does it operate only on a spiritual level? Has it a metaphysical impact of a John Donne image?

Warren returned – too soon. What feeling is created by his 'slipping' to her side, catching her hand and waiting? Is it an act in recognition of her love for himself as well as for the old man? Does she need to ask the final question of the poem? Is its unnecessary nature the reason for the economy of his reply? Is the content of his reply a surprise to us? Or have we been prepared by the imagery of the poem for the finality of Warren's utterance?

Poetic techniques

The poem makes remarkably effective use of dialogue between husband and wife exchanged in the near presence of the subject of their conversation. Their idiom defines them as simple rural folk who deal with the world on a practical level. In the wife's case, however, it is also an appropriate vehicle for the expression of sincere and tender, yet uncomplicated feeling for a fellow human being, whose demands upon her are made not by right but in consequence of their both sharing a special bond with nature.

The poem is united by a series of images relating to that universal harmony which only on special occasions may be found in existence and which binds all life together: Silas huddled at the barn door parallelling the strange hound which also sought refuge after its long travail; Harold's Latin studies pursued with the same vigour as if he were studying the violin (an emphasis on the craft and art

of language); the bonds between man and nature visually and spiritually portrayed in Silas and Harold's haymaking; in Silas's construction of the haystack in
mimicry of the birds' construction of their nests; the morning light beams'
mimicry of harp strings, themselves adorned with twinkling dew; the moon
falling and caught up by the little silver cloud and the spirit of Mary.

Particular techniques to note:

- the use of alliteration: l. 1 ('m'); l. 2 (w'); ll. 102–4 ('n' stressing the negativity of
  Silas's situation)
- the use of capitalisation and word placement: l. 2; l. 46; l. 115; l. 175
- the dramatic isolation of simple words and phrases: l. 135; l. 145; l. 153; l. 161, l.
  169; l. 175
- the terse reply pregnant with overtones of extra meaning: l. 32; l. 135; 'how
  much he's broken' (l. 154); l. 145; l. 161.
- the rhetorical parallelism and prayerful tone of ll. 102–4
- the use of enjambment: ll. 3–5; ll. 8–10
- the tactile and visual implications of 'dragged' (l. 41); 'huddled' (l. 35); 'nodding
  off' (l. 44); 'like big birds' nests' (l. 95); 'spread her apron to it' (l. 108); 'sharp-
  edged chair-back' (l. 150)
- alliteration and strong visual and tactile imagery of 'big birds' nests' (l. 95)
- the visual drama of 'part of a moon was falling' (l. 105)
- the effective use of adverbs: 'softly' (l. 107); 'gently' (l. 115)
- the glorification of the simple domestic image of the spread apron through the
  description of the light it caught
- the authentic colloquial cadences and rhythm of the speakers – capturing their
  simple lifestyle and the drama of the situation discussed between them

Themes

Consider these thematic possibilities:

- the mental and physical exhaustion of a life lived in toil
- the importance of human dignity and the price paid for it
- the limitations of what is gained by right
- the corrupting power of prestige and material advancement
- the beauty and virtue of a simple honest heart
- the power of love
- the bonds that bind all rural folk – and all humankind
- the spiritual harmony of the cosmos
- the inexorability of change and decay in the universe
- the cycle of life
- the challenges of manhood
- the weight of responsibility
- the harsh physical demands of farm life

- the poverty but generosity of rural life compared with the riches and meanness of mercantile life
- the value of true friendship and the redeeming power of compassion

Universal elements

Silas's journey is a parable of the journey travelled by all living creatures, who work, know friends, decline, suffer and die. Also consider:

- the threat to rural life of the modern forces of mercantilism and formal education
- the education to be gained from experience in the natural world in contrast to that gained from formal schooling
- the spiritual sense that pervades the universe
- the transience of all things and the inexorability of change
- the powerful negative forces of suspicion and estrangement
- the pain of isolation – the need of human beings for companionship and true friendship
- the contrast between those dues owed to others by right of kin and by right derived from the bonds of compassion of ordinary humanity
- the vastness of the universe

YOUR SECOND RESPONSE

1. Is 'The Death of the Hired Man' simply Frost's plea for human compassion, or does its message extend beyond individual relationships?
2. 'In "The Death of the Hired Man" Frost demonstrates his mastery of natural speech to convey universal truths.' Do you agree with this statement?
3. What is Frost's achievement in 'The Death of the Hired Man'? What insights does the poem give into the nature of rural existence and the natures of the rural folk who live it?
4. Is 'Death of the Hired Man' weighed down with emotion, or is its achievement the manner in which it portrays subtleties of feeling? Analyse the poem in the light of this question. Consider tone, atmosphere, idiom and imagery in your answer.

'The Mountain'

'The Mountain' develops a portrait of a rural community from its paraphrase of the two closing lines of Virgil's first Eclogue: 'And already smoke is rising from the housetop in the distance, / and longer shadows fall from the lofty mountains.'

RESEARCH BEFORE YOU READ

- Read over a translation of Virgil's first Eclogue and consider that classical poet's evocation of the landscape.
- Read Wordsworth's 'The Prelude' and note how this poet captures the sinister aspect of a mountain seen by a boy who dared approach it by boat.
- Research the symbolic connotations of rivers and mountains. What famous rivers and mountains are to be found in Greek and Roman mythology? What associations do they have with the god/s in these stories and in Bible stories from the Old and New testaments?
- Read Wordsworth's exploration of the wisdom of age and the power of water in 'The Leech-Gatherer'.

YOUR FIRST RESPONSE

A CLOSER ANALYSIS

The poem commences with an image of mystery and power: the mountain's shadow controls the town. This fact was immediately sensed even from a first cursory glance before sleep. What quality to the narrative is given by the use of 'once' in line 2? That of a fairytale? How does line 3 bring the mountain's enormity down to a size graspable by ordinary human understanding? How large does a mountain have to be to efface the western stars?

How does the alliterative use of 'b' contribute to the dramatic effect of 'cut' in line 4? Is the mountain given an evil personality by this image? Is it an actively malevolent force in the landscape rather than merely passive rock? Large as it is, does it not seem to single out the speaker for particular attention? What atmosphere is created in these introductory lines? Sinister? Foreboding? Exhilarating? Threatening? Does the shelter it provides suggest a benign being? Does the discovery of the seemingly endless fields which spread out behind the mountain portray the mountain as a deceiver? Or comforter, in its hiding from the speaker the fact of his smallness in the vastness of the cosmos?

Intruding upon his awareness of the elements of rock (built by fire) and earth is the speaker's location of the stream. In contrast to the silence of the mountain, which works on the speaker's imagination, the river is energetic and vital. It is a destructive, powerful force making its own mark on the landscape. What is the effect of the images used to portray its behaviour? Is not 'brawl' onomatopoeic and evocative of the tactile, aural and visual impact of the river? What contribution to the definition of the personality of the river is made by the vagueness of

'what it had done'? How dramatic are the monosyllabic words used by the speaker? Elemental words to capture the elemental force of water?

The river builds its own miniature mountains, and wreaks its own havoc on the driftwood. In crossing it, the speaker enters another world.

What atmosphere attends the portrait of the traveller whom the speaker next encounters? Magical? Entry into another time? Does his appearance take on a mythical quality? Is he reminiscent of Wordsworth's leech-gatherer? What do we anticipate the speaker will gain from the chance meeting? Increased awareness and understanding of life? Wisdom?

The man's message causes the speaker to revise the identity of his location. The town of his 'sojourn' was not that of the mountain – yet at night the mountain made its presence felt. The man explains that the mountain, in fact, inhibits the growth of a town. What is the implied message about human existence in his speech? That our achievements are limited by and always made in conflict with nature? That in contrast to the elements which make up the universe, humankind's achievements are minuscule and insignificant?

The image of a wall is repeated in the description of the trees. Are the trees part of nature's conspiracy against the speaker's (and all humankind's) progress? Is their hiding of the cliffs part of this conspiracy? What sense of weight is connoted by 'trunks'?

Is the fact that the ravine is dry significant? Is sterility suggested here? Danger? Difficulty?

The man dissuades the speaker from attempting to climb the mountain via the ravine. What evidence of man's rapacity or greed is given in his description of the alternative route? How is the man's expressed incapacity to be the speaker's guide to be interpreted? As deliberate unneighbourliness? As caution gained from experience? As an expression of the separateness of each individual's path through life? Does his further explanation of his acquaintance with the mountain force us to revise our earlier views of his reluctance to accompany the speaker on his journey? What mystery does he recount? Is the imagery of the icicles formed from the stream's warm breath in winter merely one of beauty? Or does it also convey violence? Evoke a nightmarish landscape? Symbolise nature's destructive power?

What is the effect of the simile? Does the comparison of the stream's breath with that of an ox magnify the stream's power? Assign the inanimate stream with a personality, a sense of being? Suggest its embodiment of the malevolent forces of the cosmos?

Still the speaker is enticed by the promise of 'a view around the world' from the top. In his imagination he makes the ascent. The realm he enters is a plane of contrasts: fragile leaves and great granite platforms; the small space of such shelves and the vast depths below them; sun and shadow; enormous mountain forms and small ferns clinging to life in crevices. Is nature's plenitude captured in these images? The completeness of creation? The variety of life and of earthly forms? Does this world take on a medieval sense as a result? A spirituality of its own? Is there not a sense of a primeval world untouched by the hand of man whilst bearing the marks of the hand of God? Eden aloft?

The man's curt response brings the speaker (and the reader) earthward to practical things – and another mystery. He has not seen the spring for himself. Is it perhaps a myth? Has it reached the status of a fable? Having eluded the climber who attempted the crevice face, is it now a modern-day fountain of youth?

Why has the man not climbed the mountain himself? Is he prevented from doing so through fear of what he might encounter? Or by a desire to preserve its sense of mystery? Has it become a sacred place for him? Is the feat too grand for a simple country man who brings in the cows and can shoot bears?

The speaker protests a proper motive for his desire to climb the mountain. Why is he so adamant that it is not merely for the sake of climbing that he aspires to reach the summit? Is his companion's revelation of the mountain's name a reminder of its nobility? What is the effect of the simile used to describe the houses. In this realm is man a special part of nature? Or is it that his endeavours are soon trivialised in the face of it?

The vagaries of the stream linger in the speaker's imagination. His companion calls its behaviour 'fun'. Why? Is it that the stream symbolises all the unfathomable mysteries of nature? How is the mystery of his own identity increased by the fact that his last word is swallowed by the air? Has he revealed too much? Or just enough? As he continues on his journey with his oxen, do we (and, perhaps, the speaker) ponder the meaning of his existence and, in particular, of his encounter with the speaker?

Poetic techniques

The language of the poem is coloured by references to the landscape: to trees and their leaves, to fern life; to granite and crevasses; to the stream and the icicles formed from its incongruous steam in winter. Is the simplicity of the description strongly suggestive of an elemental landscape still being formed by the hand that rules the cosmos?

Note the sensory range (sight, sound, smell, taste and touch) of the following images:

- the 'black body' of the mountain cutting into the sky
- the noise of the cobblestones moved by the stream
- 'ridges of sand' in grassland
- driftwood smoothed by the stripping of its bark
- the heavy breathing white-faced oxen

- the 'frosty spines and bristles' of icicles
- leafy screens overshadowing great granite rock faces
- the fragile fern fronds in crevices
- the fountain-like spring
- houses like scattered broken boulders – human scree

Themes

Consider the following thematic possibilities:
- the elusive mysteries of nature and their attraction to the human imagination
- humankind's desire to conquer and exploit nature; the thirst for knowledge
- the spirit of adventure in contrast to caution based on experience
- the necessity for each person to select and to face their challenges alone

Universal elements

Consider:
- the implacable workings of nature in the landscape – the inexorable forces of change and evolution
- the spiritual nature of the universe
- the limitations and littleness of humankind in the vast landscape of the cosmos
- nature's infinity

YOUR SECOND RESPONSE

1. Is 'The Mountain' a tale of one man's search for a good climbing experience, or is its message more confronting than this?
2. How effectively does Frost evoke the beauty, danger and power of nature in 'The Mountain'?
3. 'In "The Mountain", Frost demonstrates once again the richness of description and the wealth of meaning he can portray by means of a simple yet dramatically effective poetic diction.' Illustrate the accuracy (or otherwise) of this statement in an analysis of Frost's poetic technique in this poem.

'Home Burial'

'Home Burial' is a record of the contrasting sense of grief experienced by a husband and his wife at the death of their first child. The husband feels estranged from his wife as she rejects his desire to get on with life. She interprets his wish to do so as a betrayal of herself and of the dead child. The situation is agonising for them both. Strongly autobiographical, the poem captures the tension that existed in Frost's own marriage after the death of his son Elliott.

RESEARCH BEFORE YOU READ

- Read Ernest Hemingway's 'Hills Like White Elephants'.
- Locate the passage in D. H. Lawrence's *Women in Love* when the man upsets the woman by coming in from the graveyard with fresh soil on his boots.
- Research Shakespeare's portrayal of grief in *Hamlet* (especially in the scene of the confrontation between Hamlet and Gertrude); and in the last act of *King Lear*
- Read the biblical story of Job.

```
YOUR FIRST RESPONSE
```

A CLOSER ANALYSIS

The poem begins dramatically with the husband espying the wife as if she were the enemy and their home a battlefield. With him at the bottom and her at the top of the stairs, the stairs themselves symbolise the gap between them. Each exists on their own plane.

The wife fails to see the husband below because her attention is directed backwards – to some fear. In consequence, her step down is hesitant and hastily re-treated. What might possibly be the wife's fear? Does the poem deliberately construct the suggestion of a child. Asleep perhaps in an upper room? What atmosphere is achieved by the fact that the reader does not know what it is that specifically takes the wife's attention? What does it suggest of her personality? A certain nervousness or anxiety? Carefulness? A reluctance to leave that which holds her attention?

Her husband's demand to be told what it is that she sees from upstairs echoes the reader's own question. Note the tone in which he utters it: demanding, aggressive and dominant.

Her response is passive. Or is it defiant? Does it demonstrate her immediate withdrawal from her questioner? A silent resistance?

The repetition of the question allows the husband time to mount the stairs and stand over her. The visual image and emotional reality expressed by his posi-tion and caught in the words 'mounting' and 'cowered' is frightening– a vignette of their entire marital relationship. Is his insistence – and the tone of its utter-ance – alienating, notwithstanding the last-minute addition of 'dear'?

The wife maintains her silence. What do the slight details of her 'stiffening' suggest? A deep resolve to maintain her silence? Anticipation of physical vio-lence? The husband looks for himself. Why is it that he does not see immediately the object of her attention? What is the effect of his utterance on identification of the subject of her gaze? Is its tone conciliatory? Ashamed? Soothing? Per-plexed? Resignedly angry? Offhand?

49

Note the powerful drama accorded his statement by its isolation in the line.

The family graveyard is her husband's discovery – framed like a picture by the window. What is the effect of this image? Does it make the graveyard more personal? More significant in that it can be captured entirely in one glance? What is the effect of the contrast between the child's mound and the slabs of stone which mark the other three graves there? Is the recent event of the child's death captured by one simple word? Does the child's grave appear more isolated? Vulnerable? A barely perceptible mound in the largeness of the landscape?

Why can the wife respond to her husband's description only with the repetition of 'Don't'? Is her agony inexpressible? Do his words cause her to relive the pain of the child's loss? How raw are her emotions? How close to the surface her profound grief? Does the repetition suggest a verbal sobbing?

She shrinks from him further, her attitude emphasised by the cumulative impact of 'withdrew' and 'shrinking' and by her gesture in sliding under his arm and down the stairs. Her return look is withering. He responds to it as if it were an injustice, protesting his own right to his own grief.

She denies him this right, as she races for the door. The short sentences and the repeated 'Ohs' capture both her panic and her distress. She would have it that only a woman can properly feel the death of her child.

What is the effect of the husband's utterance of his wife's name? And of the attitude he adopts at the top of the stairs? Conciliatory? Capitulation to her anger? Confusion as to what to do next? Is the 'dear' genuinely meant? Is his tone gentle? Pleading?

Is the aggressive negativity of the wife's answer justified? Does it raise the reader's sympathy or enmity? Is the husband's plea for help from her so that he might understand all the more dramatic and moving because of her attitude?

Again, he meets her silence. Her response to his plea is to turn the latch. His explanation of his position is poignant. The perplexity her behaviour arouses in him is captured in the convolutions of ll. 57–9: 'Two that don't love... together with them.' Is his acknowledgment of the failure of their relationship suggested even as he pleads for its saving? Is there not an element of desperation in his 'Don't – don't go.' (l. 60) Is there also love? Genuine concern? Compassion?

What is the effect of the use of 'it' to name her grief in the next line? Is it so profound; so all encompassing of her psyche as to be indefinable?

What is the husband's tone and emotion as he pleads to be let into his wife's grief? How desperate is his 'Give me my chance'? Does he live out his own private agony in the face of her rejection of his love and consolation? Does she deny him the right and duty of a husband in shutting him out so completely? Where do the poet's sympathies lie? The reader's at this point? Is the husband the victim of his wife's emotional and psychological bullying? Or is she incapable of responding in any other way? Is the husband's last utterance of his plea the sneering she calls it or voiced frustration and desperation? The vehemence of his denial of her accusation marks the rising anger of his impatience with her intractability.

The wife's retort is damming: she accuses him of enjoyment of the sad task of digging the grave. Note the combined effect of repetition and enjambment used by the poet to capture the process of making the child's grave. It was a process which alienated the husband from the wife forever. Her distress and disgust were exaggerated by the small additional details of his 'rumbling voice' (could it have been gruff with suppressed tears?), by the 'fresh earth' from his own baby's grave which he walked into the kitchen, his talk of everyday affairs so soon after digging the burial plot, and his resting of the spade against the wall. Are these actions damnable as she would have them? Or merely the behaviour to be expected of a country man?

The husband's response is almost manic, so pregnant is it with anger and emotion. He sees himself as cursed.

She, on the other hand, persists in her diatribe. She recounts with disgust his remembered dialogue about the rotting of birch fences, so incongruous and inappropriate when their child's coffin lay in the darkened parlour. Did these details demonstrate as she maintains that he could not care? Or was it his way of caring? Of getting on with life in the face of his grief?

She clings to her grief and to the isolation it brings her. She refuses to allow her grief to be lightly dismissed, to descend to what she sees as a pretence. Nor will she be distracted from it by the necessary things of living people. Is not her disposition obsessive? Her total immersion in her sorrow almost manic?

In the face of the wife's passion the husband is calm. Note the controlled persuasiveness of his tone and manner captured in the short sentences. Why does the appearance of a stranger coming down the road cause him to discard this control?

She is not persuaded. His words merely add to evidence of his inability to empathise with her. Is there not blind confusion and desperation in her 'How can I make you—'?

The husband's next words are a strongly uttered warning. The rhythm of his speech is slowed. He threatens her — and faced with her silence as to where she means to go, his voice and emotions dissolve into the angry threat with which the poem concludes.

Does the reader expect that she will heed the threat? Is she not psychologically and emotionally entirely out of his reach?

Poetic techniques

The poem's title is a pun: the poem records the burial of a child at home and the burial of the couple's marriage and home life in consequence of the event. Consider:

- the power of the opening and closing words and their evocation of the enmity existing between the husband and the wife
- the dramatic effect and sense of infinitely continuing pain and hopelessness in the repetition of 'Don't', the words at once expressing the woman's pain and erecting a wall between herself and her husband
- the dramatic concentration and precision of 'Just that I see'; 'the child's mound'; 'Help me, then'; 'Don't – don't go'; 'Give me my chance'
- the cumulative effect of 'fear' (l. 3); 'terrified' (l .9); 'cowered' (l. 11); 'stiffening' (l. 14); 'shrinking' (l. 34); 'daunting' (l. 36); 'sneering' (l. 71); 'rumbling' (l. 86); 'cursed' (l. 95). What atmosphere is created by the use of these words? What is the tone in which they are uttered?
- the compassion and love of the wife captured in the image of 'his little grave' so tenderly uttered by her
- the explosive anger and frustration of the husband's final sentence

Themes

Consider the following thematic possibilities:

- the break-down of marriage – the emotional impasse between husband and wife
- the revenge taken by an emotionally oppressed wife who destroys her marriage out of frustration and anger
- the power and nature of grief
- the pain of isolation and estrangement

Universal elements

Consider:

- the pain and sadness which often characterises marriage
- the profound tragedy of the death of a child
- the destructive nature of grief
- the isolation of those who grieve

YOUR SECOND RESPONSE

1. Is 'Home Burial' too personal to be an effective poem?
2. 'The achievement of Frost in "Home Burial" is its presentation of the sustained atmosphere of animosity which is destroying the marriage of two caring people.' Do you agree? Is the poem's atmosphere its only interest?
3. '"Home Burial" has a rich and changing tonal landscape which plays with the reader's emotions.' Do you agree?

'After Apple–Picking'

This poem celebrates that special state of being of the apple-picker caught between the world of reality and the world of dream as his waking conscious-ness succumbs to the extreme fatigue his activity has caused him. As it presents the gathering of the apples it also captures the act of poetic construction. Both lead to physical and mental exhaustion. It has been called Frost's 'masterpiece' by his biographer Jeffrey Meyers in his book entitled *Robert Frost: A Biography* (Constable, London 1996).

RESEARCH BEFORE YOU READ

*   Read Keats' 'Ode to a Nightingale' and 'Ode to Autumn', rich sources of ideas for Frost's own 'harvest' poem.
*   Read the biblical story of Jacob's ladder by which Jacob ascended into Heaven.
*   Research the symbolic meanings of apples and apple trees.

YOUR FIRST RESPONSE

A CLOSER ANALYSIS

The poem commences with the strong image of the ladder pointing heaven-ward. Is the speaker's description of it as 'two-pointed' and 'sticking' an acknowledgment of it as a symbol of his intrusion upon nature? Is there a sense of violation or violence in its disturbance of the upper realm? The remaining details of the first statement complete the scene: a barrel unfilled beside it and the odd apple or two which have escaped the speaker's harvest. The tone of completion, of exhaustion of line 6 says that they will stay ungathered.

The speaker's attention moves from these physical details to the atmosphere that surrounds him. Its special beauty and sensuality is captured in the beauty of the phrases 'the essence of winter sleep' and the 'scent of apples'. All senses con-fronted and drained, the speaker slides into drowsiness. How do assonance ('e') and alliteration ('s/z') slow the metre of the poem and capture the speaker's abandonment of his self to exhaustion?

The internal vision of the speaker's imagination is haunted by the vision of the world, of another reality of a hoar-frosted world, which he viewed that morning through the ice pane skimmed from the drinking trough. How sensual is this image. It is visual. Is it also tactile? Olfactory? Auditory? The vision was only temporary as the pane melted and the speaker allowed it to fall and break.

The memory of the pane's destruction, however, does not now disturb the speaker's dreaming. Are the alternating long and short lines suggestive of sighs? Of his exhausted heavy breathing? Of his drifting in and out of consciousness as sleep overtakes him? Does the lack of end stopping emphasise his tiredness and the loss of definition for him of the boundary between a waking and sleeping reality?

How is his dream to be described? In the magnification of its apples? In its distortion of perspective? Do the russet flecks give a surreal quality to the imagined scene? His weary psyche thus occupied, the speaker retains his awareness of his physical reality. His instep arch aches yet under the remembered pressure of the ladder-round. His body, too, picks up on the remembered physical sensation of the swaying ladder.

Tiredness again intrudes upon his thoughts. As the harvest work is recalled, the poetic lines again run on and oscillate between short and long lengths. Is the onomatopoeic 'rumbling' ominous in its sound? Does this noise of the cellar bin touch the plane of the netherworld (completing the trilogy of heaven, earth and hell)? Is the rumbling an expression of nature's anger at human disturbance? Suggestive of nature's power?

What is the effect of the rhyming of lines 28 and 29? A definition of the speaker's exhaustion? Evidence of the relaxation of his mind and body, of sleep overwhelming his waking consciousness?

The speaker reviews the actual picking of the fruit, its plenteousness exemplified by the repetition of 'thousand'. The steady rhythmic ritual is captured in the short phrasing. Each part of the process – the grasping of each individual apple, the lifting it down and the guarding against dropping it –demands dedicated concentration. What is conveyed by the choice of 'cherished'? The speaker's gratitude to nature for its bounty? His communion with the creator?

Is the hasty descent of a dropped apple captured in the shortness of line 32 and its enjambment to line 33? Does the movement of the eye down the page parallel the fall of each apple?

Does 'struck' introduce onomatopoeically the sound created by the fallen apples as they strike the earth? How intrusive is its harsh 'u' and 'ck' sound on the somnambulant, soporific atmosphere of the poem to this point? Yet is there beauty in the actual details of the bruised apples and the apple 'spiked with stubble'? An authenticity drawn from real experience (of the poet as well as the speaker)? Note the viciousness of the apples' wounding portrayed in the harsh alliteration of 's' in 'spiked with stubble', its harshness exaggerated by its combination with 'p', 't', 'u' and 'b'.

The fate of the fallen apples is recounted matter of factly. The words of line 36 are particularly cold and final.

The speaker takes a step back from his imaginings to speak as 'One'. Does the use of this pronoun signpost a change of perspective from the particularly personal to the generally philosophical? Is this also the effect of the use of the subjunctive 'were'? The speaker wonders whether the sleep which he is about to enter will be human – and therefore ordinary – or the special regenerating sleep of the woodchuck's hibernation. The fact that he chooses to express this idea from the woodchuck's point of view evidences his unity as a rural working man with all creatures in nature.

Poetic techniques

Consider:

- the special resonance to the tone and atmosphere of the poem given to it by Frost's use of elevated diction
- the capturing of the rhythms of work and the numbing effect of work-derived tiredness in the long and short lines, the irregular rhyme scheme, the recurrent participles and the slow pace of the poem
- the sensuality of the diction and the imagery
- the symbolic significance of the glassy piece of ice which transforms ordinary experience into a plane of intensified feeling and awareness – a physical representation of the achievement of the poet's art
- the dream-like effect of the repetition (six times) of 'sleep'
- the powerful simplicity of the language – the easy colloquial idiom of the speaker

Themes

Consider the following thematic possibilities:

- the demands of rural labour and the physical and emotional elation and exhaustion of it as a metaphor for poetic craftsmanship
- regeneration
- the powerful effect of nature on human senses
- nature's bounty
- nature's mysteries – yet some apples escape the speaker's determined harvest
- the physical and emotional exertion which attends the speaker's gathering of the harvest he had so much desired
- the exploitation by the speaker of nature's bounty
- the individual's reality as characterised by many planes of consciousness

Universal elements

Consider:

- humankind's exploitation of nature and its greed for large harvests
- the beauty and vulnerability of nature
- the different realities which constitute the individual's consciousness

- the unity of all living creatures
- the hard work involved in rural life
- the mysteries and spirituality of nature

YOUR SECOND RESPONSE

1. Authentic images, real rituals of harvest captured in the authentic idiom of a country man. Is this the achievement of Frost in 'After Apple-Picking'?
2. 'The best poets make us see the significance to be found in simple things.' Use this statement as a starting point for your analysis of 'After Apple-Picking'.
3. Does 'After Apple-Picking' merit its description as a 'masterpiece'? Support your answer by a close discussion of the themes and techniques of the poem.
4. Compare Frost's 'After Apple-Picking' with Keats' 'Ode to Autumn'. Which poem do you prefer, and why?

Mountain Interval (1916)

'The Road Not Taken'

'The Road Not Taken' examines the difficulty that always attends making a choice between two options. It gently satirises his friend Edward Thomas's inability to make a decision and at the same time to be confident that it was the right one. It also reflects Frost's real-life experience in England in 1912 when, out walking after a winter storm, he met a man very much like his mirror image at a lonely crossroad and watched, mute, as he passed by. Frost poetically transformed the experience on converging roads to the speaker's experience of diverging roads. It was reputedly one of Frost's favourite poems.

RESEARCH BEFORE YOU READ

- Read Thomas Hardy's *Tess of the D'Urbervilles* and note particularly Tess's trek through the ancient forest.
- Read Wordsworth's 'She Dwelt among the Untrodden Ways' and note Frost's allusion to the last lines of this poem: 'But she is in her grace, and, oh, / The difference to me!'
- Read William James' *The Will To Believe*, and note Frost's allusion to James' observation that 'If we take the wrong road we shall be dashed to pieces. We do not certainly know whether there is any right one. What must we do?'

A CLOSER ANALYSIS

How powerfully visual is the first image of this poem? How important the detail of the wood's colour: its leaves yellowing in autumn?

What dramatic emphasis of the speaker's emotion is gained from the simplicity and placement of 'sorry'? And of his indecision and hesitancy by the syntax (word placement) of 'long I stood'?

What role does the enjambment play? Does it suggest the temporary suspension of time as the speaker stands and ponders his options?

Does nature participate in the teasing of the speaker's thought by the two options in the way in which it bends the undergrowth to hide the destination of one of the roads?

Stanza 2 records the speaker's separation of the roads by the operation of his will. 'Then took the other' hastens the metre of the poem – as if to suggest perhaps that the speaker made his choice hurriedly in the end, tired of the mental dilemma with which he is presented. His rationalisation of his choice occupies the remainder of the second stanza. How logical is his reasoning? Was the chosen road in reality any less used than the rejected road? Or is it that having made a decision based on the greater grassiness of the chosen way, the speaker lacks confidence in his conviction? What is the dominant tone of this stanza? Vacillating? Uncertain? Anxious? Wavering? Are not the speaker's statements in this stanza full of contradictions?

Stanza 3 rejects the tenuous distinction drawn between the two roads by the speaker in stanza 2. They were both pristine in their autumn cloak; untrodden – and therefore undamaged. What is the effect of the image of black leaves (to which their beauty will be turned by the pressure of the speaker's steps)? Is it an element of horror as well as of ugliness? A symbol of the damage wreaked by humankind on the natural world?

Is line 3 of stanza 3 a sigh of regret as much as a restatement of the choice made by the speaker? How might the exclamatory tone be otherwise explained? As the revelation of the speaker's sadness that living life involves turning down as many options as taking them up? Is the full reason for this sadness explained in lines 14 and 15? Is it the fact that any situation of choice in one's life can never be revisited? Note how in line 14 the repetition of 'way' produces an auditory enactment of the progress of the speaker's physical journey.

In stanza 4 the speaker ruminates on the future importance to him of this incident of choice. Again his sigh is foremost. The option necessarily discarded is the basis of future regret. His imagined future remembrance of the incident is cloaked in mystery and vagueness as to its own time and place: both the use of 'somewhere' and 'ages and ages' reinforces this. His future recounting of the choice forced upon him will not identify with any greater clarity the reasons for the option taken. It will merely record its consequence: '... that has made all the difference.'

Are the doubts and regrets of the past to be eventually resolved? Is the 'difference' made positive or negative? What key to the answer to this question is provided by the tone of the last two lines of the poem? Does the rising intonation of 'I' in the third last line and the gentle tonal denouement from this point of the poem's final statement provide a clue to the answer?

Poetic techniques

Consider:

- the sense of drama added to the first stanza by Frost's concentration of monosyllables and by the thoughtful placement of particular words
- the sparse but strong visual images: the two roads; the yellow wood; the leaf-strewn tracks. They provide a physical setting, a touchstone to reality against which the speaker's musings can take place. Do they acquire the significance and impact of symbols defining and extending the themes of the poem?
- the tonal quality of the poem. Is it too weighed down with sighs?
- the contribution made by end rhyme and assonance to the meaning of the poem

Themes

Consider the following thematic possibilities:

- the difficulty which often attends making life's choices and the agony of ambivalence
- the persistent sadness of regret
- the fine – and often inexplicable – choices that shape our lives
- nature's delight in mysteries and in humankind's mental and emotional discomfit
- life's continual testing of our faith in ourselves

Universal element

Consider:

- the sadnesses and uncertainties which are inevitable when an individual is not the master of their own mind

YOUR SECOND RESPONSE

1. Is 'The Road Not Taken' flawed in that its tone fails to match the strength of the challenge presented in its motif of diverging roads, or does the weak ambivalence of the speaker lie at the heart of its success?

2. Has 'The Road Not Taken' a serious and meaningful statement to make on life or does it merely deal with an insignificant incident in one individual's life?

3. Assess the success of Frost's poetic restatement of William James' observation in *The Will to Believe* that 'If we take the wrong road we shall be dashed to pieces. We do not certainly know whether there is any right one. What must we do?'

'Out, Out —'

'Out, Out —' is an exercise in pure horror portraying the bleeding to death of a boy after a buzz-saw accident. It is based on the real-life horror of the death of young man who dies of shock after lacerating his hand on a mechanical wood saw. The title refers both to the gushing of the victim's life blood from his injured man and to the extinguishing of his life.

RESEARCH BEFORE YOU READ

- Read Shakespeare's *Macbeth* and note particularly Macbeth's observations, after being informed of Lady Macbeth's death, on the meaninglessness of life.

YOUR FIRST RESPONSE

A CLOSER ANALYSIS

The buzz saw is alive and rejoicing in its own malevolence from the very first line of the poem, personification and onomatopoeia ('snarled' and 'rattled') defining its monstrous personality – and (ominously) its insatiable appetite. The implied metaphor of a vicious animal eating its fill is completed by the description of the stove-length wood sticks of its excreta in lines 2 and 3.

What is the effect of the alliterated epithet of line 3? The creation of a positive sensual atmosphere to counterbalance of the horror of the first two lines?

Is the saw's capacity to reduce forest trees to 'sticks' and 'stuff' horrifying? Nightmarish? Foreboding?

The first dangerous distraction of the saw's companion's attention is recounted in lines 4–6. How important is this description of the setting? Does

it give the saw greater reality by placing it in so specific a setting? Is even the saw dwarfed by this setting – another reminder of the insignificance of human activity in the face of the vastness of nature? The sunset brings its own beauty to the scene. We are conscious of the day's end.

In defiance of the fading light, the saw continues to devour the wood fed to it. The sound it makes changes according to the lightness or heaviness of the load it has to bear. How effectively are its efforts conveyed in the repeated phrases and onomatopoeic verbs of line 7? The alliteration of 'r', 's' and 't'? Note the additional depth of meaning provided by the contrast between the long sound of 'arled' in 'snarled' and the shorter, crisper sound of 'attled' in 'rattled'.

Are the words of line 9 ominous or reassuring? Is a growing sense of fore-boding now permeating the poem? A dreadful anticipation of a dire event? Or a false sense of relief? What is the importance of the speaker's use of 'but' in 'day was all but done'?

'Call it a day', the workman's colloquial call to 'down tools', raises our hopes that all might still be well – yet it is sadly only a retrospective exercise in wishful thinking. What would the utterance of such a cry have achieved? The pleasur-ing of the boy by the granting of an extra half hour in which to pursue the joys of youth. Are these joys all the more effectively evoked by being hinted at rather than specifically stated?

His sister's announcement of 'Supper' provokes a response from the saw which she could hardly have anticipated. Is the horror of the following event increased by the saw's personification and the continuation of the meal imagery? Does the saw react with instinctive, deliberate malice?

Why does the speaker qualify his original statement that the saw 'Leaped out at the boy's hand'? Is it that he does not want to face the unimaginable? The occurrence of the impossible? Some kind of supernatural malicious act?

Is the revised version of events: 'He must have given the hand' an attempt to rationalise the irrational? Does the use of 'however' suggest that the attempt is unsuccessful?

The meeting of hand and saw is succinctly put; the drama of the event needs no embroidery. But the dreadfulness of it!

The boy's reaction is hysterical. How could the image of his holding up the mutilated hand be described? Ghoulish? Devilish? An image straight out of a nightmare? Why is his motivation ambivalent? Is it out of shock? His own mixed feelings of horrible fear and an urgent desire to preserve his own life?

How does the boy's response change as the initial shock of the accident wears off? Is horror replaced by disbelief? Does the repetition of 'boy' increase the direness of the event? A boy's loss of his hand just as he stands on the verge of manhood? Are we held in thrall by such inexplicable and incomprehensible tragedy?

Does the speaker's use of 'all' suggest the entirety of the boy's adult experience which is now marred? Again, understatement underlines the enormity of the loss. 'Spoiled' has the ring of a child's idiom; it emphasises the youthfulness of the victim. Is not the plea that of a child for adult help?

'So' is powerful in its isolation and simplicity. Its tone is one of resignation to the inevitability of the events that follow. After all, the hand has gone already.

The cloud of ether into which the doctor puts the boy is a metaphor for the death that is soon also to envelop him. The darkness is ominous, foreshadowing what is to come.

What kind of figure does the boy make on what is to become his death bed? A grotesque parody of the energetic, beautiful young man that he once was? Are the 'puffed' lips particularly ugly? Is it the boy's last living breath which exaggerates them? Do we resist the clear message provided by these details? Do we want the boy to live? Is the reader's rejection of the awful reality of his death a parallel to the speaker's rejection earlier of the awfulness of the original event?

The realisation of the boy's passing comes in stilted moments, mirrored in the stilted syntax and interrupted metre of the poetic line. The reason: disbelief. The boy's heart stops beating; his life concludes in a simple, three-step process. The last two lines have their own horror. The boy's corpse is accorded little attention. Those still living turn to the affairs of the living. Are their actions inspired by callousness? Indifference? Or has the boy become the very picture of that fact which they most fear and wish to avoid – death itself?

Poetic techniques

Consider:

- the contrast between the noise of the saw and the tranquillity of the mountains
- the visual horror created by the blood-like behaviour of the sap of the sawn logs and its ironic mockery of the flow of the victim's life blood from his wound
- the powerful dramatic sense given to the events and to the atmosphere of the poem by the use of alliteration and word repetition
- the symbolic foreshadowing by setting of the sun of the extinguishment of the boy's life
- the drama of the victim's last moments captured in the series of short sentences which record them
- the extra malevolence given to the machine saw by its personification

Themes

Consider the following thematic possibilities:

- the dangerous relationship between humans and machines
- the hard work required of rural folk

- life's cruelties; the pointlessness but inevitability of human suffering
- humankind's exploitation of nature
- the epilogue to the events narrated in the poem provided by the last two lines
- the indifference of most individuals to the suffering and death of the individual
- the promise and optimism of youth
- the additional tragedy of the death of a young person
- the malevolent force of the cosmos which seeks out a means of self-expression
- humankind's intellectual and emotional avoidance of confrontation with mortality
- the simple events that make up a man's death
- the unpredictability of life and of death

Universal elements

Consider:
- the fragility of existence and the transience of all things
- the unpredictability of life; the role of fate and chance in our lives
- humanity's shunning of death

YOUR SECOND RESPONSE

1. Is it the realism or surrealism of 'Out, Out –' which is its chief element of interest?
2. '"Out, Out –" demonstrates Frost's mastery of poetic technique?' Do you agree? Illustrate your answer with close reference to the poem.
3. Write a poetic analysis of 'Out, Out –'.

New Hampshire (1923)

'Fire and Ice'

The poem is a concise, laconic examination of the two forces – passion and hatred – capable of destroying the world. These two alternatives are reduced to the symbols of the title.

RESEARCH BEFORE YOU READ

- Read Canto 32 of Dante's *Inferno*, a passage of which, describing the fate of sinners plunged up to their necks in ice even amidst the fires of hell, was Frost's inspiration for this poem.

A CLOSER ANALYSIS

The poem begins quietly and philosophically, the first two lines providing a balanced recognition of the role in the final apocalyptic destruction of the earth accorded to fire and ice by 'some' folk. Is the diction in both its tone and word choice deceptive in its simplicity, masking the horror of the cataclysmic events recounted in these lines?

The speaker's selection of the first alternative as his favoured means of earthly destruction is tightly and confidently uttered. His conviction as to the rightness of his choice is emphasised by the lines' rhyme, by their picking up the rhyme of the first line and by the definiteness of rhythm and of tone of the monosyllables; their evenness and assuredness disturbed only by the bisyllabic 'tasted'. What is the effect of the speaker's choice of this word? A naturalness and authenticity of idiom? Sensual colour? A hint at the self-indulgence involved in passion's fire?

The second alternative is not, however, so easily dismissed. The power of hatred (the ice) which has equal capacity to destroy the world intrudes upon the certainty of lines 3 and 4. The sound of 'ice' in the rhyme of 'twice' cuts across the strength of the sound of 'fire', an auditory overture to the statement of hatred's power in the remaining five lines of the poem. The inevitability and completeness of the earth's final destruction is caught up in the sense of finality captured in the final rhyme.

The message is ominous: the failure of one force will only ensure the operation of the other. It seems that the eventual destruction of the earth is guaranteed. And, are not these two forces different sides of the same coin of human weakness?

Poetic techniques

Consider:

* the dramatic use of understatement in the summation of the destructive power of ice and in the final word of the poem
* the sense of horror created by the coldness of the speaker's unemotional evaluation of the forces which 'some' say will account for the end of life as we know it
* the powerful resonance established by 'suffice' rhyming with 'ice' of line 2, 'twice' of line 5 and 'ice' of line 7 – an auditory resonance reinforced by the visual inclusion of 'ice' in 'twice' and 'suffice'

- the thematic and tonal strength drawn from the poet's juxtaposition of two elements each of which has the capacity to destroy a third element – the earth

Themes

Consider the following thematic possibilities:
- the power of natural elements
- human pessimism
- the ultimate inconsequentiality of human existence
- the mysteries of the universe

Universal element

This poem reviews, once again, nature's destructive power, this time taken to its ultimate conclusion

YOUR SECOND RESPONSE

1. What gives 'Fire and Ice' its special resonance?
2. 'Simplicity and economy of expression has its own dramatic force.' Is this borne out in Frost's 'Fire and Ice'?

'Stopping by Woods on a Snowy Evening'

This poem, which expresses the speaker's death wish, was allegedly the favourite poem of President John F. Kennedy.

RESEARCH BEFORE YOU READ

- Read Beddoes' poem 'The Phantom Wooer' and note Frost's allusions to its lines: 'Our bed is lovely, dark, and sweet.'
- Read Keats' sonnet 'Keen Fitful Gusts' and note Frost's allusions to its lines: 'The stars look very cold about the sky / And I have many miles on foot to fare.'
- Read Scott's poem 'The Rover' and note Frost's allusions to its lines: 'He gave the bridle reins a shake.'
- Read Shakespeare's treatment of the fascination of suicide to the man wearied by life in Hamlet's soliloquy 'To be, or not to be' (Act 3 Scene 1).
- Research the symbolic meaning of snow.

YOUR FIRST RESPONSE

A CLOSER ANALYSIS

The poem begins dramatically with the speaker's answer to an implied question as to the ownership of the woods through which he is passing. The softness of the sounds of the opening words of the first line – particularly the soft-breathed sounds of 'Whose' and the quietness of 'know' – establishes immediately a gentle, almost dream-like atmosphere which has the power to overwhelm waking consciousness. Its power is reinforced by the rhyming of the first, second and fourth lines and the alliteration of 'w' combined with the repetition of the 'dead', rather final sound of 'wood'. The setting is dominant; the speaker-traveller's stature dwarfed by the woods filling with snow.

What contribution is made to the establishment of the atmosphere by the suggestion of subterfuge in the fact that the speaker's pause in his journey will go unnoticed by the owner of the woods, who resides in the town?

The speaker's only companion is his horse. Usually representative of strength in poetry, this creature is reduced in stature, dwarfed like the speaker by the setting in which his rider has halted. How is this effect achieved? By the use of the adjective 'little'? By the attribution to the horse of a questioning of the reason for their stop? What is the effect of 'queer'? To suggest a child-like limited understanding of the situation?

What is the effect of the reference to a single farmhouse? A reinforcement of the littleness and inconsequentiality of human life in contrast to the vastness of the landscape and the power of nature? Of the isolation of the setting? And of consequent additional danger?

How does the enjambment of the lines of the second stanza contribute to the speaker's meaning? Does it capture the quizzical but single thought of the horse effectively? Is the openness of the rhymed sounds also contributing to this effect as well as to the evocation of the silence of the evening?

Is the situation of man and horse – between the woods filling with snow and the frozen lake – dangerous? Is this a visual statement of humankind's position in the universe? Caught between destructive forces? Faced with the inevitability of death?

The dreaminess of stanza 2 is disturbed by the horse shaking his harness bells. The sounds are intrusive not only on the landscape but also upon the speaker's thoughts, quite taken with the fascinating invitation to die presented by the natural world before him. Do we sense that in stanza 2, time has stood somewhat still, to start up again with the horse's reminder of his living presence? Note how the sound of 'shake' and 'mistake' is more succinct, more defined and faster spoken than the rhyming sounds of the previous stanza.

Does the gesture of the horse suggest his increasing anxiety? Perhaps at the cold now creeping over him? Perhaps at the loss of his rider in reverie?

What is to be made of the other sound? Is its singularity of reference significant? Do the adjectives ('easy' and 'downy') of the last line of this third stanza suggest the wind and snow's joint beckoning of the speaker (and the horse) to death? Does their softness make their invitation more attractive?

The end-stopping of the second and fourth lines of stanza 3 defines the horse's question and the answer given to it by the wind and the snow. Is the speaker's absence from this process significant? Is the atmosphere thereby created extra sinister? Do we wonder at the speaker's silence in response to his horse's gesture?

The first line of stanza 4 suggests the reason for the speaker's silence. In three simple adjectives the enticing beauty of the woods and the promise of serenity of their dark depths are defined. Yet their invitation to suicide is rejected in the last three lines of the poem. The speaker's journey on this particular occasion, and in life, is yet to be completed. Life – with all the exertion it requires – is to be lived rather than so easily discarded. How does the rhyme scheme and repetition capture the triumph of the speaker's will? Does it suggest a special concentration of his remaining energy in resisting the temptation for self-destruction presented to him? A deliberate application of will?

Poetic techniques

The setting of the poem with its woods filling up with snow at the darkest time of the year is heavily symbolic, representing:

* the cloud of depression which darkens the speaker's waking consciousness
* the cold dimming of consciousness which is death itself
* the temptation of suicide

Consider also:

* the lucidness of the narrative. Is it teasingly and deceptively simple, belying the significant issues it raises?
* Frost's allusion to and transformation of lines from the work of Scott, Beddoes and Keats in three lines of this poem
* the sense of drowsy dreaminess created by the use of alliteration ('d') and assonance ('y') and soft long sounds ('eas' in 'easy', 'own' in 'downy' and the 'fl' and 'ake' of 'flake')
* the contribution of the rhyme scheme to the definition of the wood's attractiveness and the speaker's determined resistance of its invitation to self-annihilation
* the contribution made to the development of the dramatic atmosphere by the simplicity of the speaker's idiom and the preponderance of monosyllables in his speech

Themes

Consider the following thematic possibilities:

- the value of steadfastness, responsibility and dedication
- the morbid temptation lurking in the human consciousness to abandon all commitment by opting for suicide
- the power of human desire for peace and security
- the strength of human will required to continue the struggle of existence rather than succumbing to the attraction of suicide
- the beauty created by the elements of nature even as they obliterate life
- the danger of the universe and its indifference to the value of life
- the simplicity and beauty of rural life
- the sense of spirituality to be found in the rural landscape

Universal elements

Consider:

- the insecurity of humanity as it confronts the largeness of the natural world
- the powerful attraction of death
- the power of nature
- the controlling force of the universe which seeks to obliterate all life

YOUR SECOND RESPONSE

1. How significant are the themes presented in the narrative 'Stopping by Woods on a Snowy Evening'? How effectively are they presented?
2. Can a poem about a death-wish really be called great? Discuss the themes and poetic techniques in 'Stopping by Woods on a Snowy Evening' to support your point of view.

West-Running Brook (1928)

'The Bear'

'The Bear' contrasts the freedom and confidence of the bear's existence with the physical and psychological 'caging' of man and his confused existence between science and philosophy.

RESEARCH BEFORE YOU READ

Research the life and habitat of the brown and grizzly bears of North America.

A CLOSER ANALYSIS

The bear's portrait is presented in the first twelve lines of the poem. Its great strength is captured in the first powerful visual and tactile image. What does the simile suggest of its personality? Does this image also cleverly introduce the second subject of the poem – humankind? Is it an image suggestive also of nature's abundance and sensuality? Is 'snap' onomatopoeic, adding the sense of immediate, present, real experience to the scene described?

What significance can be attached to the fact that the bear is 'she'? Does it explain the passion of her embrace of the tree?

The next image captures in auditory, visual and tactile terms the bear's great strength. What is the purpose of the aside? To extend her personification established in the first lines of the poem? To parody womankind's similar exertions?

Does the barbed wire introduce a sinister note? Is it more than a statement of the bear's physical power that she so ably clears this barrier which seeks to circumscribe her ramblings? Is it significant that the bear leaves behind a lock of hair? Is it a talisman? A statement to humanity that she will not be so easily confined? A symbol of the harm humans do to their fellow creatures?

The rhymed words ('staples' and 'maples') at once capture, in the balance of their two stresses, the momentary teetering of the bear on the wire, and the swaying of the wire released from the bear's weight.

How beautifully does the image of the bear's disappearance down into the maples complete the poem's evocation of the mountain landscape to this point? Has the poet cleverly conveyed a sense of its great heights and depths?

The effect of line 10 is to turn the previous narrative into a fable of freedom. Lines 11 and 12 explain its advantage over us and the confinement of our own lives. Does the rhyming of these lines give the statement they make the power and certainty of a universal truth?

The simile of lines 13–15 ascribes to humankind the behaviour of the poor caged bear. Does the use of 'poor' establish a tone of sympathy for this man's dilemma? Is his 'nervous inward rage' deserving of sympathy?

The rhythm of line 16, the swaying sense created by the two conjunctions assigns to the caged man a mental and physical loping parallelling that of the caged bear. The onomatopoeic 'click' of his toenail against his cage and the onomatopoeic 'shuffle' of his feet dramatise the self-imposed imprisonment of his mind as it oscillates between the world of science (symbolised by the microscope) and the world of philosophy (symbolised by the telescope). 'In conjunction' they cover the universe but what is it that they give humankind? Confidence? Anxiety? Confusing messages about the nature of existence?

Confusion is the message of the description of the man's behaviour as he rests from his scientific pursuits to ponder the 'two metaphysical extremes' each of which vies for the attention of his intellect.

Is the man parodied in his confusion by Frost's use of the phrase 'on his fundamental butt'? Does the image and its humour demonstrate Frost's lack of patience with formal education and his lack of respect for the joys and revelations which it might bring? Is the bear metaphor taken to absurd extremes in this and Frost's subsequent observations?

Frost finds that he is unable to resist the friar-like vision his imagery has evoked. The rocking motion of the man conjures up a clear picture of his use of his buttocks – and is syntactically and metrically conveyed again by the conjunction of short phrases and the use of repetition.

His love of Greek learning is woven into the poem; the parallelism of the lines suggesting rhetorically the fine balance between the credibility to be given to the scholarship of one Greek scientist/philosopher as against that of the other.

The final image is clownish, the portrait of a rather decrepit animal such as one might find in a circus.

Poetic techniques

Consider:
* the contribution made to the meaning of the poem by the contrast that is established between the bear and human beings
* the controlled metaphorical parallelism between bear and man, and man and bear
* the contribution to the meaning – and humour – of the poem of syntactical (grammatical) and metrical structure
* the raw colloquialism of 'fundamental butt'

Themes

Consider the following thematic possibilities:
* the intellectual confusion of humankind which is founded in learning
* the majesty of the wild bear
* the value of the simple, natural life lived by the bear in contrast to the limitations of the more sophisticated life of humans

Universal elements

Consider:
* the lack of freedom of humankind in society in comparison with the freedom of creatures living in touch with the natural world

- the insignificance of humankind in the universe for all its so-called intellectual superiority
- the shallowness of human learning when set against the profundity of existence
- the insignificance of individual lives – humankind or beast

YOUR SECOND RESPONSE

1. 'Frost's close observation of animal and human life is illustrated in "The Bear". It has the strength and interest of authenticity.' Do you agree? Refer closely to the techniques as well as the themes of the poem in your answer.
2. A dislike of academic scholarship and a dislike of his fellow man. Are these the main themes of 'The Bear'? What ideas does Frost present in his poem and how well does he present them?

A Further Range (1936)

'A Lone Striker'

'A Lone Striker' condemns the harm done to the individual's psyche and dignity by the machines of industrialised society. Against the soullessness of mechanised life it presents the freedom and psychological attractiveness of a simple rural lifestyle. Given the power of the controllers of industry and the cruelties they are prepared to inflict on their workers, the striker's escape to the preferable reality of the natural world, is a heroic – but futile – protest at the dehumanisation of the world.

Frost writes from experience as, in 1891, he worked in Braithwaite's woollen mill, where six days a week, he collected empty thread bobbins. As a high school graduate, he also worked as gatekeeper at the Everett's woollen mill. It was his job to shut the entrance against those men who were late for work. Their fine was a half-hour's pay.

RESEARCH BEFORE YOU READ

- Read Thomas Hardy's poem 'The Darkling Thrush' and note Frost's allusion to Hardy's lines: 'The tangled bine-stems scored the sky / Like strings of broken lyres.'

YOUR FIRST RESPONSE

A CLOSER ANALYSIS

The poem begins with the energetic rhythms which invigorate its narrative. The bell is a strong symbol of the paramount importance of time in the regulated life of the mill worker. Its 'tolling', onomatopoeically conveyed, adds a funeral element to the poem's atmosphere.

One worker fails to enter the mill gate on time. Note the rocking rhythm of the pronouncement of his sentence, and the elevation of his crime's significance by the reference to the 'law of god'.

Does the rhyme of 'ock' not give the judgment passed an awful sense of finality? The consequences for the man are profound – rebuke and unemployment. Is the fact that their elaboration takes the space of only one line significant? Is this an implied judgment of the amount of attention or worth which the industrial bosses accord any one individual worker?

His enemy is the mill. Is its description metaphorical? Suggestive of a Gorgan-like creature? A titan? What is the effect of the image of its 'many-many' eyes? Emphasis on the mill's monstrousness? Ugliness? Symbolic of its unrelenting supervision of its workers? Is the opaqueness of the eyes suggestive of deception? A veil of secrecy? The death of life inside?

Is the suggestion that a machine might stand 'forlorn' for the lack of the man's attention a statement of the man's own sarcasm. Is it also Frost's? Does the personification of the machine by the use of this adjective suggest the power which the machine has over the lives of those workers who tend it? The physical and emotional demands made by it? The man's bracketed thoughts are angry, bitter, sarcastic.

Despite the fact that he is shut out, the man can imaginatively reconstruct the activity inside the mill. The alliterative use of 'f' reconstructs the dustiness of the air. The slowed pace of the diction of line 20, in particular the demanding stresses of the monosyllables in the first half of the line, capture the tension of the stretched woollen yarn, its steady lengthening echoed in the lack of full end-stopping of lines 19–22. The yarns' importance and resilience is caught up in their personification. They are safe, cared for tenderly by their human attendants.

Are the workers equally safe?

The break in the rhythm of the spinning caused by a break in a yarn is captured in the rhyming couplet of lines 24–5, and the curtness of the rhymed sound.

Second to all the lines devoted to the description of the machines and the yarns they spin comes the description of the human spinner and her deft hands. Is the harp simile appropriate? What is its effect? An ennobling of the spinner? A commentary on the pride which she takes in her work? A suggestion of some mystery she evokes in making the threads blend? A statement of the validity and positive importance of her role?

The striker rejects the message of his imagined vision for a more favoured 'other place'. What is the effect of the initial vagueness as to the identity of this place? Do the images evoke a sense of a lost Eden? Is the striker's desire to stand among the lofty trees on cliff tops, to be enveloped by their branches, indicative of his desire to escape? For the emotional and psychological security which can only be achieved by pastoral life? Does the use of feminine endings in lines 40 and 41 animate this natural landscape?

Refusing to allow his immersion in the natural scene to remain the stuff of conjecture, the striker strikes out firstly imaginatively and then actually to a find that realm. The feminine endings and progressive aspect of 'walking', 'drinking', 'thinking', 're-renewing', 'talking' and 'doing' enact grammatically and rhythmically the energy he hopes to find there. There he will be the active controller of the events of his life rather than a passive responder to the needs of a machine. He will be rejuvenated.

Having made the decision to embark upon his journey of renewal, the striker can afford to be more generous in his thoughts about the mill. His wish for its 'modern speed' is a rejuvenation of the old cliche 'God speed'. His deviation from the usual saying is explained in his next observation: the mill, after all, is not divine.

He recognises its power, however, (even if arrogantly) with the assurance that should he be specifically needed by the mill, he will make himself available. The irony of his self-deceptive confidence in his own self-worth is highlighted by the fact that he says that as he leaves and would still say the same in the future. The reader knows that he will never be called back to work. Has he not opted for a life that is passing? Of decreasing significance and importance with each passing year?

Poetic techniques

Consider:
- the use of personification to animate the mill to the level of a fit adversary for humanity
- the use of feminine endings and variation in rhythm
- the (misplaced) cockiness of the striker's tone in the last section of the poem

Themes

Consider the following thematic possibilities:
- self-preservation
- the material and social prosperity of the strongest and most resilient individuals
- the futility of rebellion and social protest
- the loneliness and estrangement of the dissenter

- the pleasantness and freedom of a life lived in touch with nature in comparison with the confinement of a life lived according to the strict work code of industrialised society
- the inevitable triumph of industrialised society over the pastoral world
- nature's power to rejuvenate the human spirit
- the individual human being's insignificance set against the vastness of the natural world

Universal element

The poem exemplifies one incident in the evolution of society and the inevitable domination of human beings by machines.

YOUR SECOND RESPONSE

1. Is 'A Lone Striker' too proletariat a poem to hold much interest?
2. '"A Lone Striker" is at one and the same time, the nostalgic expression of the desire of a young Frost to escape the demands of working in Everett's mill and a parable of the triumph of industrial society over the pastoral world.' Do you agree? Consider in your answer, the authenticity of the imaginative worlds evoked in the poem

A Witness Tree (1942)

'The Subverted Flower'

'The Subverted Flower' is strongly autobiographical. It recounts the deception and pressure Frost placed on Elinor to give in to his passion before she was ready to do so. The encounter of the poem's subjects is not mutually gratifying and scars the woman's psyche forever.

RESEARCH BEFORE YOU READ

- Read John Donne's 'The Flea' and note the argument that the speaker of this poem uses to bend the woman's will.
- Read Andrew Marvell's 'To His Coy Mistress'.

YOUR FIRST RESPONSE

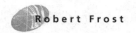

A CLOSER ANALYSIS

The simplicity and brevity of the opening phrase of the poem capture at once the young woman's tentativeness and her innocence. Her nervousness contrasts dramatically to the self-control of the man. The balance in the metrical divisions and syntax of the line captures the opposition of wills. What is the impact of 'lashed'? Does it hint at the man's deviousness? The urgency of his lust? Is the offering of the flower an inversion of Eve's offering of the apple to Adam?

Is his smile sinister? Her response predictable? Is his reaction to her un-responsiveness revealing of his character? And of his ruling emotions? What is the tone of the alliterated words 'flicked' and 'flung'? Is his distaste and anger captured in the curtness of the sound?

Metaphor and simile combine to state the truth of the seducer. He is animal-like in his passion.

She stands like a modern day Venus, surrounded by nature's beauty. Is this why he hesitates to touch her neck and hair? Is his control of her total at this point? Is she transfixed by the demands of his masculinity? By his smile?

The man is tiger-like. What does this image and the details of the heaviness of his breathing reveal about the passion within him? That it is barely controlled? Note the support of the imagery by the onomatopoeic verbs. Is the effect one of ugliness?

Is the statement of her avoidance of him all the more powerful and mean-ingful because of its brevity? Is she repelled by him?

Why does she resist the urge to run? Is she fearful of attack? Of his brutish response?

Her mother's call intervenes into the dramatic silent tension of the moment, and yet increases her fear. Might it not precipitate him into action?

The man's response is a mix of passion and shame. Which emotion prevails? The girl blames the flower for her predicament – but is not the secret yearning in her own heart also to blame? She 'saw the worst'. In him? In herself? Is this her recognition of the ugly reality of lust?

The metaphorical comparison of the man to a beast is extended into the description of the man's hasty – and cowardly exit. How dramatic are the visual images of his flight? Has the control he first exhibited totally abandoned him? Is the use of 'bark' appropriate or unnecessary use of onomatopoeia?

With her seducer at a safe distance the woman is able to vent her feelings. Does the vehemence and nature of her tirade not demonstrate that the incident has defiled her? Will she ever be the tentative creature she was at the start? Or was this beast lurking in her as well? What does the foam at her lips suggest? Her actual physical deflowering?

Poetic techniques

The poem makes effective use of contrast between the man and the woman, between the man's control and loss of it, and between the woman's innocence and loss of it.

Note especially the extended metaphor by which the man's animal lust is defined and the woman's awakened.

Consider the sense of inevitability of events provided by the use of rhyme, short lines and hastening rhythm.

Themes

Consider the following thematic possibilities:

- the brutal passions which are the basis of man's – and woman's – character
- the ugliness and energy of lust
- the power of shame
- the understanding between women of their common suffering at the hands of men

Universal elements

Consider:

- the age-old war between men and women
- humankind's animal instincts which belie any superficial sophistication

YOUR SECOND RESPONSE

1. How effective is the imagery, rhyme scheme and line length of this poem in conveying the drama of human passion?
2. Analyse Frost's portrayal of human lust in 'The Subverted Flower'.

Steeple Bush (1947)

'Directive'

'Directive' deals with the sacramental and spiritual importance of poetry and the value of locating the poetry that is within us if we are to be regenerated.

RESEARCH BEFORE YOU READ

- Read Wordsworth's sonnet 'The World Is Too Much With Us' and note the similarity of theme to Frost's poem.

- Research the significance of the search for the holy grail in Arthurian legend and medieval literature.
- Research the significance of the Communion in Christianity especially in the Last Supper. Note especially Matthew 26:27–8 'And He took the cup, and gave thanks, and gave it to them, saying, Drink ye all of it: For this is my blood.'
- Read Mark 4: 11-12 'All these things are done in parables: That seeing they may see and not perceive.'
- Read T. S. Eliot's 'The Waste Land' and note his emphasis on the search for the holy grail.
- Research the symbolic meaning of water.

YOUR FIRST RESPONSE

A CLOSER ANALYSIS

The poem's beginning is beautifully evocative, beckoning in the quietness and serenity of its tone the reader's consciousness back to the past. The sense of falling back in time is conveyed especially by the concentration and definition of the verbs of line 3, the repetition of 'house', 'farm' and 'town' echoing the mind's struggle to resurrect lost images, and the simile of the graveyard sculpture dissolved by the weather just as inexorably as past reality is dissolved by time. How could the atmosphere created by these images be described? As surreal? Misty? Dream-like? Spiritual? Morbid?

What is the effect of the personification of the road? Is the reader entering a nether world? Another plane where skeletal kneecaps pave the way and where there is a danger of becoming forever lost? Does not the road gain a mythical significance in its having been recorded in a book and in its having been subjected to and having survived the vast movement of the glacier. Does it not bear itself the scars of experience? Do not its own wounds record the malice of nature and the suffering which is always part of existence?

How dramatic is the personification of the glacier? Does it not assume the imaginative proportions of a titan scouring the earth for its own idle amusement? Is this the reason why his ghost still lingers? Is he drawn uncontrollably to the scene of the suffering he has initiated? Is his return another crossing of the barriers of time? From the past to the future?

Do the references to the 'iron wagon wheels' and the glacier not sustain the sense of retreating backwards into time?

What is the significance of the naming of Panther Mountain? Does the name itself reinforce the motif of nature's destructive power? Does it also provide the reader with a much needed touchstone to reality in the midst of confused time?

What are the eyes that watch? The organs of fantasy creatures watching he who walks by with intense interest? And with intense suspicion? Is the choice of 'ordeal' meaningful? Is this an Arthurian journey? A re-enactment of Sir Gawain's quest for the holy grail? And what of the woods' reaction to one's passing? Personified, they are hideously animated, seeking to frighten rather than to sustain. Note the intrusion of the sound of their rustling leaves on the traveller's (and the reader's) consciousness, a sound captured by assonance, alliteration and personification.

Why were they not all there twenty years ago? Has time's passing brought the speaker/traveller to a greater understanding of the nuances of life, to an appreciation of a spiritual world which is inaccessible to youth? Has time's passing provided the hours and days required for a conquest of the simple reality of 'old pecker-fretted apple trees' by cosmic forces and creatures which prey on life?

How is the traveller to succour himself? To maintain his self-control in the face of such a nightmarish landscape? By a song which seeks to recapture the innocence of the road now walked and of the pastoral life once lived there? Is the possibility of the presence of a fellow rural worker or of a buggy load of grain up ahead comforting? Or further discomforting in that they might be ghosts?

The high point of the road is the boundary between two cultures now lost. It is also a platform from which the traveller can stake his claim to whatever is left. What is the effect of the poem's change of vision from a horizontal to a vertical plane? Does the image thus created call on our memory of fantasy worlds in the skies of childhood fairytales?

From this vantage point, the traveller can see that man's mark on the landscape has almost been obliterated, reduced as it is to a field whose size is defined in a beautifully simple rural image, a children's cubby house, a few china remnants lying below it. Why are these fragments particularly poignant? Is it that they symbolise the innocence of childhood? Its simple needs and aspirations which contrast so profoundly with the sophisticated desires of adulthood?

If this is cause for weeping, how many more tears are elicited by the ruins that were once the traveller's home? Is it the familiarity and simple domestic life lived in that home that is captured by the simile? The practical, honest lifestyle that it fostered?

What is the effect of the speaker's juxtaposition of 'destination' and 'destiny'? Is it to emphasise the focus of the journey? What is the symbolic significance of

the brook which is so determinedly sought? And of its gentle character, its rejection of the raging habits of brooks less lofty and less 'original'. Why 'original'? Is this the mystical source of all life? The brook that fed the Garden of Eden? The fountain of youth?

The goblet is hidden – it is the speaker's own grail. What is the significance of the fact that it is broken? Why has he placed it under a spell? To exclude non-believers from partaking of this special, rejuvenating communion? The barbarian with no creative or imaginative spirit? The agnostic? The undeserving? What is the significance of the goblet's origins? Is it only through the eyes of a child that we can ever hope to understand the mysteries of the universe, and to enter the kingdom of heaven? Is it only to true believers in the mysteries of existence that salvation and regeneration of the spirit are accessible? The last two lines celebrate this fact in a tone of religious fervour which recalls the Christian Communion service.

Poetic techniques

Many of the poem's central themes are developed from biblical allusion so as to emphasis the poet's main thesis that poetry is the new religion and, like the old, only accessible to those who are true believers.

Consider also:

- the powerful symbolism of the holy grail
- the strong visual and auditory images which define the fantasy world, the faerie land through which the speaker must travel to find his holy grail, and the magical waters which will refresh his being
- the sacred tone of the last lines of the poem which recount the traveller's achievement of his purpose
- the physical and imaginative planes through which the images of the poem transport the reader – the poetic definition of the spiritual dimension, of the land of the imagination

Themes

Consider the following thematic possibilities:

- the importance of the past and the survival in memory of its most important incidents
- humankind's search for truth and meaning
- the redeeming quality of purity
- the religion of imagination/poetry
- the power of memory and of the mind
- the importance of locating the poetry within us so that we might share in its life-saving qualities

- the degeneration and decay of all things
- the power of the destructive forces of nature
- malice and suspicion as cosmic forces with which humankind must contend in the imaginative (or actual) journey through life

Universal element

The poem celebrates the power of the human imagination to create its own reality and to return to the source of life so that the spirit might be refreshed.

YOUR SECOND RESPONSE

1. Is this poem one of Frost's greatest? Is it in this poem that he taps the source of all of poetic inspiration and its importance to human life?
2. Examine the impact and significance of the imagery of this poem as it develops the poet's themes.

In the Clearing (1962)

'Pod of the Milkweed'

Many critics consider this poem a masterpiece in its depiction of a catastrophe as thousands of butterflies, drunk on the sweet honey and bitter milk of the milkweed, beat each other to death in a frantic but hopeless struggle for survival. Only one of their number survives. This ballad demands the reader's confrontation of the dreadfulness of life.

RESEARCH BEFORE YOU READ

Read Exodus chapter 3 verse 2 and note Frost's allusion to 'a land flowing with milk and honey'.

YOUR FIRST RESPONSE

A CLOSER ANALYSIS

The poem begins loudly with its colloquial calling of 'all butterflies'. The reference to 'race' in line 1 establishes at once the speaker's metaphorical use of the butterflies as symbols of humankind – in fact of the fate of all living things. What

does the mystery of their source suggest? Their universality? The undiscoverable secrets of nature? Is the fact that their source is 'no special place' a statement of the butterflies' representative quality?

The butterflies are 'ever' caught up in the rituals of their lives. Unlike the bees, they have no secure place, no home. They are drawn inexorably to the speaker's door by the milkweed. What is the message that their coming brings? The wanton waste of life that is part of nature? The waste of nature's war against itself? What is the effect of the alliteration of 'w' in 'wanton waste'? And of the choice of adjective? Do both suggest nature's unscrupulousness? The immorality of the disrespect of the ruling cosmos for the sanctity of life?

So profound an event is that which a flower initiates in the speaker's backyard that it demands to be told in song to all the world. Are the butterflies' ennobled in consequence of the fact that their fate is made the subject of ballads?

Is there a biblical resonance (an implied metaphor of angels, perhaps?) in the speaker's description of 'the countless wings', 'the infinite' and the 'noiseless tumult'? Do not the juxtaposition of the weed's plainness and singularity and the butterflies' ornamentation and multitudinous numbers symbolise visually the range and plenitude of creation? The co-existence in the cosmos of the malign and the benign, of evil and good, virtue and innocence? The mysterious counterbalance between nature's impetus for creation and for destruction? Is the repetition of 'drab' needed to counter the intensity of colour provided by the butterflies?

The combination of the superficial suggestion of goodness in the milk of the weed and its deeper malignancy restates in the one symbol the same duality of mature. This malignancy pours forth when the weed is wounded. What does this personification of the milkweed contribute to the image? An emphasis on the active enmity of the milkweed? A conscious endangerment of other life? Does the milk's suggestion of opiate speak of the supernatural bond between all evil things of the cosmos? What is the effect of the accumulation of taste references? And tactile images? A dramatic definition of the central concept of poison? How richly sensual is the imagery of the poem as the weed's viciousness is exposed?

The butterflies are fatally tempted by the promise of honey, indifferent to the deaths of individuals amongst their number. They mutilate others, knocking the dyestuff from their wings. Their thirst is akin to lust.

The scene of the massacre of the innocent insects has yet its own surreal beauty. The taste, touch, sight, sound and smell of it is portrayed in the image of the dust cloud thus created. The weed has pulled off a masterful deception on this one day of the year. What nobility and pathos is given to its victims by the references to their damaged 'regalia' marred even on the day of their gaining it and by the comparison of their wounding to that which is self-inflicted by the fruitless beating of one of their kind against the window pane?

The first line of the second section provides the answer to the reader's unspoken question as to the purpose of such destruction. How satisfactory is this answer? Is the service of waste in the world as significant in nature as procreation? Is life to be sacrificed in the service of so little point? What is the gift of the 'restless dream'?

Why is the pod personified? Its imagery is grotesque in its reference to 'talon feet'. Is its significance thus enlarged? Its symbolism of the reality of evil in the universe more clearly defined?

What is the pod's final message to humankind? That the waste and malice of the universe must be faced 'fairly' and squarely? That we cannot evade the dark side of existence? The alliteration of 'f' makes the tone of this final statement insistent, coldly matter of fact – as confrontational as the ideas and images of the entire poem.

Poetic techniques

Consider
- the butterflies' symbolism of the fragility of all life
- the pod's symbolism of the ugliness, evil and ruthlessness of nature
- the dramatisation of the confrontation between butterflies and the weed by the use of personification
- the poet's exploitation of the imaginative power of juxtaposition
- the powerfully sensual imagery
- the sense of fatalism and inevitability given to the events described in the poem by the poet's narration of them in ballad form
- the confronting tone of the poem's conclusion

Themes

Consider the following thematic possibilities:
- the co-existence of forces of good and evil, of creation and destruction in the universe: the duality of the cosmos
- nature's lack of conscience
- the place of waste in nature's universal scheme
- the reality of evil
- the power of instinct and of lust
- the equal significance of beauty and ugliness in the natural world
- the deceptive nature of appearances

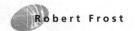

Universal elements

This poem celebrates the ever-present cruelty and waste that characterises nature's dealing with the individual lives of creatures that are its being. It confronts the human desire to find a purpose in everything, revealing that meaningless waste and suffering is part of the nature of things. Is not the butterflies' experience a metaphor for human experience?

YOUR SECOND RESPONSE

1. How would you define Frost's achievement in 'Pod of the Milkweed'?
2. Is nature's waste of life at the heart of 'Pod of the Milkweed'? Is the poem entirely depressing?

5

Preparing successfully for exams

Using quotations effectively

A successful discussion of poetry requires an effective illustration of its use of language and imagery in creating its atmosphere and in developing its themes. This can often be achieved only by the integration of quotations into your discussion. Effective use of quotation will demonstrate an awareness of the following points:

- Short, direct quotations, included in quotation marks and fluently integrated into your own discussion, are usually the most effective.
- A full stop is placed at the end of a short quote if the sentence ending coincides with the end of the quote. Otherwise, the punctuation of the sentence which contains the quote is uninterrupted.
- Short quotations should not be indented as this practice will interrupt the flow of your ideas.
- Quotations of more than two or three lines should be indented so that they are visually distinct from the text of your discussion. Indented quotations do not have to be included in quotation marks. To continue your discussion after their use, you should start the next line of your writing against the left margin.
- Long quotations can be abbreviated by omitting words and replacing them with an ellipsis (…), the standard indication of an omission. Make sure that the words you do include contribute to and follow the context of your discussion.
- Any adjustments to a quotation to fit the context of your own discussion should be included in square brackets: [ ].
- Any explanation of the quotation's meaning or relevance to the argument, if included within the quotation, should be enclosed in parentheses: ( ).

Remember that quotations should enhance your discussion and illustrate or assist the development of your argument. They will not save a weak argument or replace your own effective discussion of ideas.

Some tips for exam preparation

As you prepare for poetry examinations, remember these points:

- Follow the syllabus and gain a working knowledge of each poem set for study on your course. Do **not** try to second guess the examiners as to the individual poems they will ask you to write on, or the features of them they will emphasise.
- Give some structure to your revision of each poem by organising its themes into a hierarchy of significance or interest. Do not feel obliged to discuss each poem in the same depth, but do note the development of the theme throughout the poem.
- A fully effective discussion of themes requires you to examine the techniques of language (including assonance, alliteration, rhyme and metrical patterns) and imagery used to develop them.
- Identify the pattern of imagery developed in the poem and note its expansion of the poem's ideas.
- Identify any symbols used by the poet and the range of their possible meanings.
- Consider how the atmosphere and setting of the poem contribute to its meaning and to the conveying of the poet's message.
- Consider the sounds of the poem – poetry is, after all, sound with meaning

As well as studying the poems, make time during your preparation to polish up the basics of essay structure. You exam answer should by restricted to a range of properly illustrated points in an essay which has an effective introduction, inter-linking paragraphs each developing one major idea, and an effective conclusion. This is a good start to earning high marks.

Don't overburden yourself with quotations, and remember: answer the question!

Exam topics and guides to answers

Many examiners invite you to choose two or three poems to illustrate the achievement of the poet selected for study. You should prepare for this contingency by knowing all the set poems well, including their themes and the poetic techniques used to develop them. Always try to write in an informed way as much about the language of any poem as its ideas. **Never** learn only two or three poems and trust that the examiner will allow you to choose the works which are to be discussed. The examiner is perfectly within his/her rights to select particular poems for your analysis.

Sometimes the examiner will provide a specific viewpoint from which the poet's work is to be analysed. Also be prepared, therefore, for selective discussion of the set poems. A successful response to this type of questioning will often require you to leave out as much as you put in your discussion of any particular poem.

Set out below are some topics to provide you with practice in this more focused critical approach.

Topic 1

What is the quality and nature of Frost's poetic achievement? 'Terrifying' as Lionel Trilling once called it? Worrying in its portrayal of a cosmos in which malice prevails? Dogged by a sense of the futility of all existence? Support your point of view by the close analysis of at least two poems.

CHECKLIST

In answering this question, you might like to consider:

- **'Mending Wall'**: the bloodlust and primitive superstitions and suspicions of primitive man live on in modern man; the continual battle which humankind has with nature which seeks to destroy whatever it builds.
- **'After Apple-Picking'**: the mind-numbing attraction and power of sleep; our battle against that exhaustion which saps our strength and weakens our waking consciousness; an enactment of our resistance to the abandonment of all consciousness in death; the mysteries of existence which continue to tease our reason and test our emotional, psychological and physical strength; our exploitation and waste of nature's resources.
- **'The Road Not Taken'**: the terrifying reminder of the anguish of our many moments of indecision and of the possibility in all our lives of lost opportunities; the need to rationalise the paths our lives have taken.
- **'Out, Out –'**: the active malice of the cosmos confronts us in the bloodlust of the buzz saw as an ordinary day's work is turned into a nightmare.
- **'Stopping by Woods on a Snowy Evening'**: the power of death and the weakness of life; the attraction of suicide as an escape from the toils of existence; the energy and power of the annihilating forces of the cosmos.

Topic 2

Is it the authenticity and vigour of Frost's spoken rhythms which are his greatest poetic achievements?

CHECKLIST

In answering this question, you might like to consider (in addition to the discussion of the diction of each poem elaborated on under the heading 'Poetic techniques'):

- **'The Road Not Taken'**: the speaker's confusion captured in a confessional tone which nevertheless captures his anguish at having to make a decision and accept its consequences; the poem is full of the sound of sighs.

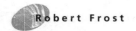

- **'Stopping by Woods on a Snowy Evening'**: a poem of atmosphere which presents the most disturbing proposition – that of suicide – in the simplest narrative.
- **'Out, Out –'**: a marvellously rich tonal landscape transporting us through the sense of foreboding brought by the darkening sky, the dreadful delight of the buzz saw in its job; the intense shock of the accident; the victim's hysteria followed quickly by his desperate fear; the helplessness of the onlookers and then their indifference.
- **'Fire and Ice'**: a superbly and worryingly confident statement of universal truth about humankind's capacity and potential for destruction.

Topic 3

'Frost's images are highly memorable and effective in fostering the development of his themes.' Do you agree? (Refer to at least three poems.)

CHECKLIST

In answering this question, you might like to consider:
- **'The Bear'**: the comparison of human behaviour as that of a caged bear in the confusion suffered as a result of learning.
- **'Out, Out –'**: a poem full of the images of nightmare: the bloodied, mutilated hand, the gushing blood, the snarling buzz saw animated, it seems, by its own bloodlust; the indifferent rolling mountains of Vermont; the collaboration of the darkening sky in the murder of boy.
- **'Fire and Ice'**: powerful visual and tactile symbolic imagery defining the destructive potential of humankind's most primeval passions.
- **'Stopping by Woods on a Snowy Evening'**: the numbing coldness and awful beckoning beauty of woods filling with snow at evening; the gentle figure of the horse alive with the desire to live.
- **'After Apple-Picking'**: the variety and beauty and plenitude of nature symbolised in the apples gathered by the speaker; the evocation of orchard life; the three realms of existence: heaven, earth and hell.
- **'Mending Wall'**: the detailed delineation of the wall, the poem's central symbol; the murder of the hare; the pleasing patterns of the rural landscape; primitive man poised to strike his neighbour.

Topic 4

What insights do Frost's poems give into the human heart and the demands of ordinary existence?

CHECKLIST

In answering this question, you might like to consider:

- **'Out, Out –'**: records the mortal effect of shock; enacts in the speaker's response to the victim's death and, in the details he provides of the victim's reaction to the loss of his hand and of the observers' response to his last moments, the primeval fear of death; the shallowness of most individuals' feelings for the suffering of others.

- **'The Road Not Taken'**: the power of regret; the anguish attendant upon decision-making for some people; the need for self-justification.

- **'Stopping by Woods on a Snowy Evening'**: the powerful attractiveness of suicide to the exhausted traveller; the inner urge for rest; the element of escapism in our subconscious.

- **'Mending Wall'**: the ancient enmities which lie embedded even in the modern human heart; human bloodlust; the power of suspicion.

- **'After Apple-Picking'**: the escape of the subconscious to the plane of dreams; the intuitive response to the mysteries of existence.

- **'Fire and Ice'**: the threat that human passions and hatreds represent for the continuity of existence.

Topic 5

Frost's poems provide a picturesque bestiary which reflects his close observation of animal life. Are the images he conveys of our fellow creatures merely of picture-book interest?

CHECKLIST

In answering this question you might like to consider:

- **'Mending Wall'**: the hunted hare whose fate illustrates modern humanity's primitive bloodlust; the yelping dogs who represent the active malice of the universe.

- **'Stopping by Woods on a Snowy Evening'**: the speaker's horse whose harness bells are the only intrusive sounds in the deadening quietness of the woods filling with snow; its symbolism of the vulnerability of individual life in a vast universe governed by forces indifferent to its fate; the shaking of the harness bells is an instinctive response of the horse to the presence of death; an expression of fear which makes its own contribution to the poem.

- **'After Apple-Picking'**: the speaker would seek the woodchuck's wisdom as to the rejuvenation he may achieve in the sleep that is overwhelming his waking senses; the woodchuck has special knowledge of this and is, like the apple-picker, a participant in the mysteries of existence which are part of a life lived in close association with nature.

- **'Out, Out –'**: the buzz saw is personified as an animal of prey seeking out the boy's arm to satisfy its bloodlust; a powerful symbolism which transforms the saw into the representative of all the destructive forces and active malice of the universe.

Topic 6

Discuss the major themes of Frost's work and evaluate the success of the poetic techniques he employs in their presentation.

CHECKLIST

In answering this question, you might like to consider:

- **'Mending Wall'**: the irrational clinging of humankind to the false boundaries and unjustifiable certainties which divide one individual from another; the alienation and estrangement captured in the very ordinary act of two neighbours restoring the unnecessary stone wall between them in the face of all the cosmic forces which seek to level it; powerful images of human savagery (past and present) and repeated platitudes extend the thematic range and development; the mysteries of existence are interwoven into accurate details of pragmatic rural life.
- **'Fire and Ice'**: the inevitability of the earth's destruction succinctly expressed through dramatic symbols of humankind's two most destructive emotions: passion and hatred; the symbolism gains extra depth from its archetypal, primitive nature; the confidence of the speaker in his assertion and the completeness of the destruction of all known life is also captured in the rhyme scheme.
- **'Out, Out –'**: a sense of immediacy and an intense reality given to the poem's exploration through one incident of the presence of evil in the world and of the horror of the death of one young man; all our senses are assaulted – by both the powerful images and the use of onomatopoeia as part of the poet's full exploitation of the sounds and the rhythms of colloquial idiom.
- **'The Road Not Taken'**: the difficulty of decision especially for a prevaricator captured in the finely balanced imagery of two roads.
- **'Stopping by Woods on a Snowy Evening'**: the attractiveness of suicide captured in a powerfully symbolic setting which is deceptive in its beauty. Is self-annihilation really so very attractive? The enormity of the universe and the vulnerability and insignificance of individual lives presented in the juxtaposition of the tiny figures of the horse and the speaker against the obliterating whiteness of the snow.

Topic 7

Does the country base of Frost's poems limit their significance?

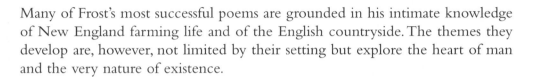

Many of Frost's most successful poems are grounded in his intimate knowledge of New England farming life and of the English countryside. The themes they develop are, however, not limited by their setting but explore the heart of man and the very nature of existence.

CHECKLIST

In answer this question you may like to consider the following:
- **'Mending Wall'**: the vigour and interest given to the poem by the authenticity of its setting; Frost's intimate understanding of the workings of frost and ice; the implied pun on the poet's own name; the illustration of human cruelty in the behaviour of the hunters; mending a wall in farming country as a metaphor for the continuation of all human enmity and separation; the exploration of metaphysical themes of nature's destruction of human achievements and of its promotion of the egalitarianism of all living things; the illustration of the forces at work in the cosmos.
- **'After Apple-Picking'**: the powerful sensuality of the images and again, the authenticity of the setting; the poem's statement on the beauty and variety of nature; the resonance given by the symbolism of the apples; the evocation of a dream-like state; the parable of regeneration through acquaintance with nature presented through the experiences of one apple-picker; the evocation of the realms of existence: sky, earth and netherworld – the stuff of myth.
- **'Stopping by Woods on a Snowy Evening'**: the evocation of the atmosphere of a special place at a special time; the presentation of the attraction of self-annihilation.
- **'Out, Out –'**: a rural accident takes on metaphysical significance; the poem's interest lies heavily in its portrayal of the physical, psychological and emotional reality of horror and its impact on the human psyche, and in its success at making the reader confront that which he/she most wishes to avoid – death.

More focus questions

Here are some more focus questions for you to use as a starting point for your own analysis of Robert Frost's work. (You will find some clues to help you to formulate your response in the previous material. Remember, though, that a well-informed and thoughtful, original response, supported by close reference to the text of your selected poems, is always the best.)
1. 'Poetry is the exploration of intense experience.' Discuss this statement with reference to Frost's work.
2. 'Frost develops individual characters in specific situations to make statements of universal significance.' Is this the basic strategy of Frost's poems?

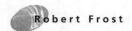

3. Is Frost essentially a pastoral poet, at home with rural folk but ill at ease with non-rural folk?

4. Spirituality is an essential theme in Frost's work. Illustrate this fact by reference to at least three of his poems.

5. To what different realms of social and personal existence are we transported in Frost's work?

6. What is Frost's view of the cosmos and of humanity's place in it? Illustrate your answer by reference to at least three of his poems.

7. Select two of your favourite poems and analyse their representation of Frost's poetic theory. (Refer to biographical notes.)